PUSHED TIMES, CHEWING PEPPER

Sarah's Story

Myra Jolivet

Pushed Times Publishing, LLC.

ISBN: 0990803201
ISBN 13: 9780990803201

"Pushed times make a monkey chew pepper."
(Challenging times inspire unique actions).

—Creole Proverb

Acknowledgments

I had some of the best advice in the writing world in trying to birth my first novel. First, I would like to thank Roger Paulding for his tough-love coaching and patience; Max Regan for his unique ability to know your characters as well—or better—than you do; Joanna Shearer, an author, teacher, and editor whose instruction was invaluable; Pat Getter for proofing with her sharp eye for detail; and author Andrea White, who pushed me into the deep end of the pool so I would swim. I would also like to thank my patient first readers: my big sis Lorraine Jolivet-Quinn, Jerome Gray, Pat McFarland, Richard Fernandez, and Gail Brown; my other big sis Linda Jolivet, a librarian, who gave me exposure to librarians, book fairs, and clubs; and my talented brother, Fred, who can also tell a great story. I am grateful to the people who make me believe I can do all things: Esther de Ipolyi, Marlene McClinton, Rick Kaplan, Suzy Bergner, Ar Lena Richardson, Jan Buckner-Walker, Paul Wood, and my new author friend, who should bottle her energy for sale, Pamela Samuels-Young, whose gentle shove brings inspiration. There is a Source of my imagination, which enables me to do all things.

Thank you also to the ones who left the nest and inspired me to reclaim my life and talents, my amazing, rock-star children: Dr. Samuel Washington III and Shelby Washington, MBA.

And finally, thank you to my parents, Nancy and Douglas, and all of those Creoles who filled my life with "warm, crazy" and made this story and other stories possible.

Prologue

Fear makes you count sidewalk cracks like a sugared-up six-year-old. I was filled with it as I walked the brittle sidewalk near Tenth Street and University Avenue. It was an area of Berkeley, California, that was not the Berkeley the world knew. There were no signs of social activism or environmental justice. The people who walked these Berkeley streets walked in survival mode, head down, witnessing nothing. The streets were trimmed in urban blight and neglect. A microphone intimately taped to my lower body could have been a gun for my tastes, but it wasn't. It made the crotch of my pants hang funny. I found the correct address. It was a crumbling two-story wood-frame house that looked like it should be condemned. I took a deep breath and walked up the concrete steps. It wasn't the kind of place I would ever live and certainly wasn't where I intended to die. How did I become a police decoy for a crazy person, like some played-out movie plot? This was the clichéd birth of my new life. Problem was, the old life had to pass on and I was the one to bury it. My walk of survival was not in avoiding the truth any longer. I had done that for about a year. My walk now was full-faced into all of the signs and visions I had ignored, into the unsafe spaces of my nightmare.

CHAPTER ONE

I *f I didn't think it would make a few bitches in the family happy, I would jump from this damn window. Talking to my cousin Stacy always made me feel like that. But therapists who kill themselves don't get clever epitaphs, just pity.*

I am family therapist to the crazies while my screaming knuckles grip my own sanity tightly. I am Sarah Doucette Jean-Louis, the face of Louisiana ambiguity in looks and life. I am a California native with Louisiana roots. That part is not unique. I'm like hundreds of thousands of Louisiana black Creoles whose families migrated to California after World War II, the liberal state with plenty of jobs. And they had kids like me, aware of the culture but tired of it. My life is one big gumbo. My family and friends come in all colors and races, and my love life has had a few ingredients added that, like a gumbo recipe, should remain secret. The unique thing about me is that I inherited the gift of *visions*. I see into the future, I guess. It's difficult for me to accept that the mind movies that come to me in a fit of nausea and head spinning hold prophetic value. But as Aunt Cat says, "We Creoles got plenty *mystevious* gifts, yeah." Her word for mysterious. I keep looking for books to help me with this, but, at this point, I haven't found any that are as specific as I would need.

"Jean? Jean?"

Jean, my receptionist-assistant, appeared in the doorway, slender in her perfectly pressed, every-short-coiffed-hair-in-place way. She was wearing one of her favorite pantsuits. I hated pantsuits—too matchy-matchy. I intentionally mixed up the jackets of my suits, even if they were the same color.

"Yes, Dr. Sarah? What is it?" she asked.

"Talking to Stacy always throws me off my game. She bragged about her husband and offered sympathy that I didn't have one yet. Is this a contest? She needs to focus on her life. She pretended that she needed to talk about that God-awful family reunion coming up next week, but it was an opportunity to screw with me." I stopped myself short of the neck-rolling anger that was building in my body. Stacy had been pushing my buttons since childhood.

Jean was apologetic.

"That's why I almost didn't put her call through. I know how she upsets you, but she said it was important." She pursed her lips in a look of guilt and irritation.

I loved to say shocking things to Jean. "No problem. One day, I'll kill her…Kidding."

She did her predictable gasp and then shook her head and smiled.

My cousin Stacy was a good Creole, unlike me. She perfected the art of marrying. Every good Creole woman had a husband. And the cultural mainstay was that every woman should strive to get her MRS, and my PhD just didn't cut it with my family without a husband to add to my CV. The great man-grab was the oldest and most enduring family competition, which I never seemed to win.

Jean's voice faded into the background as a numbing throb rocked my head. The room swayed, and all I could see was a flash of jagged colors. A knife-sharp pain pierced the point between my eyebrows as I was hit by one of the colorful flashes that preceded my visions. The sensations appeared without warning in visual language. In this one, I saw a dark room. I was dancing alone. Then I was in a bridal gown that had blood pouring down the front of it. I tried squinting to make the picture clearer, but it wasn't connected to my eyesight. It vanished, as always. Aunt Cat said I was lucky to have inherited the gift of vision, as she had. But Aunt Cat knew how to use and interpret what she saw. I just became confused. I had spent many years trying to find an explanation for the images that popped into my mind with physical symptoms. For most of my life, they were infrequent, but as I grew older, I noticed an increase in

2

visions both while sleeping and awake. Could this bloody wedding gown have been a testament to my horrendous track record with men? *Who knows?*

My attention returned to the room and my sore temples. I tuned in to the muffled words of Jean.

"Dr. Sarah. Did you hear what I said?"

"Oh, sorry, Jean, I was just looking out at that pretty blue sky." I noticed the familiar figure on the street. Between the street vendors and pedestrians was one of my scariest patients, Mr. Corwin. Mr. Corwin had progressed from overly interested patient to full-fledged stalker over the past six months. He was creepy, but I had taken an oath to help the creepy and the undesirable. It was my work. I wanted to help connect Corwin to that better part of him, his spirit purpose. My friends wanted me to dump him.

"Oh my God, why is Corwin standing down there again looking up at this window? And wait till you see today's headwear, Jean. I have got to drop him as a patient one day. Does he have an appointment?" I asked.

"Yes, in about three minutes," Jean answered, checking her watch.

"Is it my imagination or is he lurking around outside of our office more lately?" I asked.

"Yes, he is. This crush on you is becoming out of control. I think you need to send him to another therapist. I really believe that." Jean rolled her eyes up to their familiar spot on the ceiling as she backed out of my office, closing the door behind her. She took her place at her desk, ready to greet lurking, stalking Corwin.

I hated to leave my view of the gentrified downtown Oakland. I enjoyed staring at the lines of the new buildings snuggling between remnants of older, rougher times. I heard Jean knock as she walked back into my office.

She announced Mr. Corwin. "Your three o'clock came up to the mountaintop."

I stretched out a sarcastic smile in Jean's direction.

"Oh, joy."

"I'll get him," she said.

When the door reopened, in walked the man who lived his life in that space between genius and bonkers. I could see Jean struggle to control a smile as he made his grand entrance. Corwin marched into the office, straight and tall, as if he were leading a parade. The blazing-red child's bicycle helmet on his head made me think of those circus elephants. Corwin believed that wearing hats protected his brain from bad thoughts and strange voices. While he took several minutes to decide which chair to sit in, I nursed my insecurities, which had reemerged with Stacy's call.

Maybe I really should be married. I am forty. Maybe Ma-ma is right and I do have a problem with men. Who knows? That gorgeous guy who's been coming to the club lately, Mr. "Oh-I'm-Fine," could be the one.

I stopped thinking about the gorgeous man of my dreams to give my attention to the wacky one in front of me. Corwin touched each chair as if it were on fire.

Please pick a chair and sit down.

I didn't feel like dealing with Corwin. I had to search for my professional composure.

"Good afternoon, Mr. Corwin. How are we today?"

"Well, I have to say, I am struggling." He crossed his legs, and I could see black pantyhose covering his anemically pale legs. Corwin was dressed in a beautiful gray suit with a white shirt and maroon tie. If it weren't for the child's bicycle helmet and the pantyhose, he could have passed for a sane businessman—or just sane, period. But Corwin was not able to hold a job or a business. His wife supported him. The fact that she married him probably qualified her to join him on my couch, but who was I to judge love? In my professional opinion, she did not want to admit she made a mistake in marrying Corwin. I also wondered if she feared he would become violent if she did leave him.

"So let's pick up where we left off and talk about why you are struggling," I said.

My practice was based on the Carl Jung philosophy and the belief that everyone has a spiritual purpose and that purpose is essential to his or her well-being. He also believed that all of us have shadows in contrast to our conscious personality. Mr. Corwin was a white male

4

whose shadows stood erect in the face of his so-called "normal life." While he whined, I looked past him and his crooked circus helmet to the window behind him and the sky I cherished. But his annoying, copper-tinged voice brought my eyes back into the room.

"The voices are stronger than ever, Dr. Sarah. Every time I think I'm doing better, they contact me and tell me to do crazy things." Corwin's voice was in his regular singsong. "But I think I need bigger hats so I don't listen to them and don't give in. I don't want to do the things they want me to do. I mean, sometimes I *do* want to do the things they tell me to do, but when they tell me to do them…"

Holy Fridays.

I let Corwin talk, as we therapists do. Then I suggested that he begin to journal everything the voices told him to do. I figured that if he was dangerous, this might be used as evidence, as I feared that Corwin might one day take out his entire family. He was a soft-spoken deviant whose eyes could go from warm to chill in seconds. The one-hour session with Corwin felt like three hours.

"I'll see you next time. In two weeks." I breathed out in relief.

"Yes, unless you need to see me more often?" He had the usual hope in his voice.

"No, every two weeks will do. And we don't like it when you hang around outside of the office. OK?"

I was firm. He ignored me. He stood up and marched out of my office with the same pomp and Sousa of his entrance. Jean saluted once he had cleared the door. But her laughter soon melted into serious concern. She shook her head from side to side.

"I like this less and less."

"It happens. The therapist can often become the object of attention or even—yuck—affection," I explained. I secretly thought to myself that if I had to be plagued with the Louisiana weirdness of visions into the future, they could at least tip me off as to when Corwin would blow. What the hell good were my visions anyway?

Three patients and an hour of paperwork later, it was five o'clock, and I was one step closer to Saturday and the chance to possibly meet the good-looking man I had my eyes on. The weekends were my time to indulge in my passion of singing. It began as a way to make extra money, but I kept it up because of my love of music and access to men. The club at Marlin on the Bay at the Berkeley Marina had become my man laboratory. Unfortunately, the two men I had dated from my man lab were both duds. Leo was one of them. He overcologned and wore cheap suits. Frank, who supposedly was not involved with anyone, had a violent girlfriend. One night, the girlfriend had followed us. We were about to walk into a movie theater when a car screeched up to the curb and a heavyset woman, ghetto-fabulous with curvy, long red nails, jumped out of a sputtering car. She was wearing a flowered muumuu covering orange leggings and wiggling to balance in black stilettos.

"Frank! Frank!" she shouted as she walked toward us.

"What in the hell are you doin' with this bourgeois heifer? You tryin' to be all high class now? Humph. Don't she know you not available?" She grabbed Frank's arm and turned to me.

"And you! Get ya own man, if you can. You need to stop trying to be white, and maybe you'll get a black man. Humph. Don't know what anyone would see in you anyway..." She pulled Frank into the car while she continued to call me names. Her comments eventually trailed off into a series of "humphs."

Onlookers applauded. I retreated in Chanel-wearing high-class humiliation. He never showed up again after that. Good riddance. So much for the man-lab part, but it made for entertaining stories to laugh about with my girlfriends.

Once at home, I began to shake off the week and to plan what I would wear to perform with Chico on Saturday. I opened the refrigerator and honed in on last night's steamed vegetables. I nuked the whole dish and took them into my bedroom while I searched my endless racks of outfits. I decided to up my courage with couture so that I would have the nerve to talk to the cute guy. I was a therapist stereotype, like the cobbler's wife who had no shoes. I encouraged others to move beyond their fears, while I hid behind my own. It was time to take some of my own advice. It was time to take my most feared step and actually flirt with a guy first. It was so difficult for me to do sober. I feared rejection like arachnophobes feared spiders. It was time for an important breakthrough for me and my social life.

Chico flung his pink boa over his shoulder and hammered the piano. He played the intro to my song three times because I was distracted and didn't pick up his cues.

He whispered, "Start the song, shit!"

"Calm down," I answered.

Chico was a gifted piano player who had never formally studied music. We were a pretty hot attraction at Marlin on the Bay. The restaurant overlooked the bay and had a bar area and dance floor.

"OK, OK. I'm ready now," I told Chico. He didn't know it, but my eyes were on assignment, searching every corner of the room to see if the guy I wanted to meet was there as he had been several weekends over the past couple of months. I hadn't told Chico what I was doing because he had lost patience with my crushes. Our first song was Nancy Wilson's "Guess Who I Saw Today?" It was nearly perfect, not Nancy Wilson-perfect, but pretty close. I had studied voice and classical music as an undergraduate before I dove into psychology at Berkeley. One issue I recognized in my own life was that I had studied life more than I had actually lived it. I encouraged patients and friends to come out of their comfort zones, search for their internal wisdom, and take huge faith leaps. But I didn't. I played it safe in my romantic life. It didn't work for me, but I couldn't help myself. I had a classic fear of confrontation and rejection. I would later learn that constructive confrontation and the courage to face possible rejection actually helped to build healthy relationships rather than end them.

I tapped Chico on the shoulder.

"He's here! He walked in, and I have officially stopped breathing." My chest heaved.

"Is this a new crush? I am so sick of you looking at men from afar and being too chicken to say hello. Here's you: 'Is he here? Oh, there he is! Oh, is he coming?' Girl, this time go up and introduce yourself on the next break." Chico shook his head while fanning his jeweled index finger and boa in frustration. I did a hard whisper so our conversation wouldn't be picked up by the open microphones.

"Why should I have to go up to him and say my name? He should come up to me."

"Do you know how silly that sounds?" Chico spit the words out, and they managed to sound comical. He actually reminded most people of the late comedian Richard Pryor.

"What, silly? I don't want to make the first move. I'm the girl." The comment rushed from my mouth before I could catch it.

"Yeah, it's so much better to stare at him. All you need now is to hang your mouth open and drool, and you make the whole package," he said.

"Smartass."

"Dumbass," he shot back.

"I love you, you no-piano-playing bag of wind," I sneered.

"Love you back. And shit, if I could sing, you wouldn't have to show up! Now, let's entertain these people." Chico flashed a smile at me.

"Let's." I smiled back.

Chico and I had become like sister and brother—or sister and sister since he was flamboyantly gay. His taste in clothing could be considered urban confusion. He often had to explain why many of his bold patterns should be worn in the same room, let alone on him. But we teased, taunted, and insulted each other in fun.

We started the next song. A wave of something powerful blew through the room. The crowds parted—not really, but it seemed that way to me as he walked from his seat to the men's room.

This time, when he looks at me, I'll engage his eyes, smile, and whisper hello. I'll try to have swagger. Not easy for me, but I'll try it out.

It took all of my courage, but I looked directly into the eyes of the bookish Adonis. He locked eyes with me for a long minute. He smiled and mouthed, "You're great." At least that's what he seemed to say as he returned to his table. I was cool; he was cool. That is until I saw him reach for a table to break his fall. He had stumbled while walking away. Guess those heavy-duty eyeglasses needed updating.

OK, not exactly smooth, but still handsome.

I grabbed the microphone and used it to steady my nervous hands. Chico's loud piano and the hum from the crowd calmed the nervous vibration in my chest. Four songs later, my dream man walked to the side of the stage to talk to me.

"You have a great voice. Contralto?"

"Yes," I squeaked, while the richness of my voice became impoverished.

"It is not my intent to interrupt your set, but I had to compliment you on doing a wonderful job with difficult songs. And you are a beautiful woman," he said.

He was right. I thought that I looked pretty hot in my lavender vintage gown with a flower in my hair. But it was kind of corny that he would use the word "set," like he was all into the music scene. It was a little Sammy Davis Jr.–groovy. But he was talking to me, so c'est la vie.

"And who would you be?" I asked.

"I am Dr. Lance Gaston."

Ah, hell, another French name. Did every African American in California have to have Louisiana Creole roots? I guess it was either Louisiana or some other slave ship docking point in the South. But…did he just say doctor? Oh, hell yes! I could see Ma-ma calling all of her friends pumped with pride, and the cherry on top would be making Stacy jealous! Oh yeah, this could work!

"Glad to greet you, Gaston." I couldn't resist the alliteration. My eyes shyly looked down and then stuck on his shoes.

Are those tassels on his shoes? Good Lord, my dreamy man is looking more like a nutty professor than a Denzel.

His nerdiness was funny to me, and I had trouble hiding the tiny smile that wrestled with my upper lip. He saw it, and his eyebrows spiked with confusion.

"What's so funny?"

"Nothing. I'm glad you like the way I sing," I covered.

"I have been noticing you for a while," he flirted.

"Really?"

"Yeah. I like this place. I like the entertainment."

"Thank you. I like an audience who appreciates my show," I flirted back.

"Maybe I can buy you a drink later?"

"I would like that. We break again in about fifteen or twenty minutes."

One martini later, Lance and I were sitting at a table near the stage area, expanding on our introduction. We exchanged histories and business cards.

"I moved to the Bay Area to join the pediatric department at Helmington hospital in Berkeley, and I just bought a home in north Oakland," he explained.

"You grow up around here?" I asked, now with a regular heartbeat.

"No. I am originally from Sacramento. I missed out. You make Oakland look good."

"Thank you, again. I actually grew up in Berkeley, but Oakland is home, too." I was feeling much more comfortable. Thank God for vodka. I soon learned that my dream guy was not a god among men, but rather a human man who loved telling his own story—a lot.

"I went to Houston for my premedicine work at Rice University. After that, I went east to Harvard Medical School. I spent a few years in Chicago and Los Angeles, but I had always planned to return to the Bay Area. It is home to me now."

No wonder he talked like a textbook. My friends and I had gone to some pretty heavy-duty schools and a few went Ivy League, but this guy was so Harvard. He had a tendency to overenunciate, and he limited his use of contractions. He wasn't my usual type of man, but I was strangely drawn to him. I was usually attracted to smoother guys who were a little slick, but there was something about this one that I couldn't explain.

"This area is hard to beat. It has it all…" I was beginning to launch into the Bay Area boasts of great weather and proximity to skiing and beaches, but Lance's attention was diverted and he abruptly cut me off. He stood up and offered me his stiff hand like an insurance salesman.

"Well, it was great meeting you." He sounded scripted.

What a bastard! It was like cold water doused on my hot dream. I didn't know whether to be insulted or pissed off. I chose both and held my hand out with the same businesslike chilliness.

"Uh...uh, sure. It was great meeting you, too." I had to hide my anger and disappointment.

Man-bitch. Why come over and talk to me, get all friendly and flirty, and then just go cold? I don't get it.

I followed Lance's gaze and realized that his group of friends had arrived. The group included a white woman with strawberry-blond hair and a kick-ass body that she made more obvious with a powder-blue skin-tight, all-in-one catsuit. It seemed to be made of one of the new spandex-blended fabrics because it hugged her curves more kindly than leather would have. The party also included two other men, possibly colleagues from the hospital, one black, one white, and both with dates. I guessed the strawberry-blonde was Lance's date because she immediately kissed him on the cheek. My heart sank. I had waited weeks to meet this man only to crash and burn the first time we connected. I wore the look of the defeated and walked back onto the stage. I stood next to Chico to reach for my sweaty glass of water and to wind up our show.

"Are you ready to sing, or are you just gonna suck from that glass? You may not need the cash from this gig, Mz. Girl, but I do!" Chico chastised me softly.

Chico didn't know what had happened. It would have pissed him off, and while I had rejoined him on the stage, my earlier spirit had not.

Here I was again falling for another unavailable, bullshit man.

I pulled my shoulders up and back, put the drink down, stood up, and remembered that I was a hot woman wearing expensive clothes.

"Yeah, I'm ready," I responded to Chico, a bit dazed.

"What did that Negro say to you?"

"It's OK. He didn't say anything."

"Somethin' took the sparkle from you. Sarah, what did he say? I will hurt his fine ass!" Chico put his hand on his hip, poised for a fight.

"No. You know how these things go. You don't really know people." I didn't complete the thought or the sentence, but Chico accepted my answer.

I saw him lean to look toward Lance's group. I could tell from his face that he noticed the date. My mind quickly began to deconstruct my invented life with Lance in our renovated Victorian house with two girls attending a posh private school. My mother would live in the garage apartment, serving as part-nanny, part-critic. I gained control of my daydreaming mind and belted out "Stormy Weather." The audience stood up with applause.

My eyes had wills of their own and refused to stop glancing at Lance's table. He never looked away from the woman who touched him often on his arm or leg.

I closed my eyes through the remaining songs in order to make their table disappear. When the show ended, I collected my well-worn sheet music.

"Fuck him. At least this time, Chico, I learned early."

"That's right, girlfriend. His loss."

I squeezed Lance's business card, which hadn't left my hand since he had given it to me, knowing I had just lied to Chico and myself. I had a feeling this was not really the end of Lance. I knew there was more to come. I just didn't know what.

Where are those damn visions when I need them?

CHAPTER TWO

The loud ringing of my cell phone woke me up and caused me to make that hiccup sound that happens when you snore and choke at the same time. It wasn't early by my standards, just about 9:00 a.m. on Sunday. I searched the nightstand for the phone and trailed my fingers past the empty bottle of fine cabernet that had followed me to bed. I figured it was my mother or one of my girls. I had an eclectic group of longtime friends I shared laughs and fights with at our customary martini brunches or lunches, or as we called them, blunches. The term fit for those days when we stayed in a restaurant so long the two became one and we became blitzed. I was more playful than annoyed as I answered the phone.

"Who is this on a Sunday-morning-after-I-sang-last-night?" The voice that replied to my sleepy taunt was neither my mom's nor one of the girls'. It was mellow and male.

"Well, I did not know the rules. I will never call on a Sunday-morning-after-you-sang-the-night-before again," Lance mocked me.

I sat up in bed shocked, while I tried to sound more alert.

Thank you, God, for my intuitive gift.

I started to straighten the top of my taupe silk pajamas and the bed linens as if he could see the room over the phone.

"Oh. I thought you were someone else." I managed to talk over my escalated heartbeat.

"Evidently. How are you this morning, Sarah Doucette Jean-Louis?"

I cleared my throat. "Fine and you?"

13

"Great. I am calling because you have an appointment with this doctor. Me. Can I take you to dinner this weekend, or do you have to work at the restaurant?" Lance asked.

"Actually, singing at Marlin's is just a hobby. My main work is my family therapy practice." I felt obligated to clear that up although I had given him my business card. "I would love to have dinner with you, but aren't you dating the woman you were with at the restaurant?" I managed to hush my inner bitch and took the edge off my question.

"I had a date, but we are not dating," he said.

Heard that before.

"Well, I'm not big on going out with somebody involved in a relationship. But thanks, anyway." I was chilly and dismissive.

"No. It is not a relationship, believe me. Some of my colleagues introduced us, trying to matchmake. She is not a girlfriend. It is not a match. That was my first and last time out with her. They meant well, but I was not really into her." Lance almost pleaded.

My happy, light feeling returned.

"Well, if that's the case, I guess dinner this Saturday is OK," I said.

"Where would you like to go?" he asked.

"Well, Sky restaurant in downtown Oakland is great. Have you been there?" I shook my hands to work off the nervousness and tried to slow my pulse.

"No, I have not. I need to be introduced to the fine-dining haunts. It took you no time to suggest a place, so obviously, I have the right guide."

"I do love fine food. I think Sky is the perfect first stop on the restaurant tour."

Restaurant tour? Oh my God. I sound like a nerd now too.

"OK, Sarah. I will make the reservations. What time shall I pick you up?" he asked.

"I think seven will work. I'm in the condos on Jayne Avenue, off Euclid near Lake Merritt. I'll e-mail the directions to you. I still have your card with your info. It's pretty easy," I said.

"And it sounds very close to my house. I am not far from the Lake Merritt area myself. But send the directions, just to be sure. I have to

14

go to the hospital this morning. So, see you Saturday. I am looking forward to it, Sarah." He hung up.

"Are you that gullible? You should have gotten more proof of his situation." Nikeba was dunking a cherry in and out of her mimosa by its curved stem. She was my closest friend, but the attorney in her too often showed up in our girl brunches, lunches, and blunches. We didn't get together every weekend but at least once a month—either Saturday or Sunday—and more often when either of us had an emergency to talk through. I had decided to wake up the girls to meet for a late-morning Sunday mimosa brunch and talk about the new man kind of in my life.

"Proof? How exactly is she supposed to manage that with a new guy?" Sandy asked.

Sandy took her usual opposite position to Nikeba's. Sandy, short for Sandra, was our more sensitive member.

"Let's go over this." Nikeba was talking with her hands as if she were in the courtroom and I was on the witness stand.

"You saw the guy out with somebody. He knew you would see him with the girl at Marlin's, but now he expects you to go out with him? What kind of man brings his date to a place where a woman he wants to date sings? I say, cancel." Nikeba tossed back the last of her mimosa and motioned the waiter for a refill.

"Nikeba, for all he knew, Sarah could have been in a relationship or married or not interested. And for all you know, his friends could have insisted that they go to Marlin's." Sandy sounded annoyed. She was sensitive but could be firm and always stood up to us when she disagreed.

"OK, I realize that I provide you *married* women with good material, but let's move on. I wanted opinions, not orders. I've decided that I will go out with him. I just have a good feeling about him." I raised my fluted glass in a fake toast.

Nikeba rolled her eyes in disgust.

"Well, just let us know where to meet for martinis when you find out he's an Ivy League jerk." She closed the subject.

"Be more positive, Nikeba. Sarah should take some risks. She has never followed her own advice. Sometimes playing it too safe keeps you out of the game," Sandy insisted.

"That's it. No more Lance-talk. Move on, nothing to see here. What's going on with you boring married people?" I teased, and we talked until the lunchtime waitstaff had taken over.

You would think the people at Chalice restaurant in North Oakland would be used to us by now. It was one of our regular spots, but we would catch stares from other patrons when we became loud and animated. We sat outside until our sun-soaked buzzes signaled the time to go home. My friends balanced out the incompatible family I was born into, and, healthy or not, we were committed to our routine visits of philosophical discussion, laughs, and drinks. Although I was laughing with the girls, inside, I was truly concerned and nervous about going out with Lance. Was he a player in nerd's clothing? Was I too eager to meet a Mr. Right? At this point in my life, my win-loss tallies in dating were toppling over on the loss side. I didn't need another bad experience.

What the hell is going to happen? I had a whole week to worry about it. *Ah, shit.*

I spent the entire week before my first date with Lance rehearsing our conversation over and over in my head. At one point, I even acted out the date at my dining room table, changing chairs as I switched roles. I had become my mother. She acted out scenarios. *Troubling.*

I didn't tell Jean about my upcoming date, but I knew she suspected something because I was happier than usual, whining less and bouncing more from Monday throughout the week.

"Dr. Sarah, you seem really happy. You usually hum and smile this much when you have a date." Jean smirked as she stood in my office. She had waited until Wednesday to ask. I didn't want to jinx the date by talking about it, but I was feeling pretty good, having nabbed a date with the gorgeous doctor. My face was blowing my secret with a cool, fixed smile. Jean had noticed it, of course.

"I have a date with him. I have a date this weekend with Lance, the fine guy from Marlin's!"

"I thought so." Jean clapped her hands in excitement, genuinely happy for me. "I really hope everything works out." She walked toward the door to get my appointment.

"We'll see."

I had work to get through and two and a half more days, so I reined in my imagination and forced my mind to shelve Lance thoughts until the end of the week. Before I could pick up my next file, my stomach turned with bitter-tasting nausea and my head was swimming in dizziness. I held my desk to steady myself. A vision appeared. I was in bed, and the bed was moving, but not really going anywhere. It seemed to be moving in circles. I looked a bit like Dorothy in *The Wizard of Oz*, on this traveling bed. Like thin smoke, it vanished. I sat down and pulled out my journal. *I have got to crack the code of these things. It's obvious they will be with me for life, and they are increasing.* I went to the master, Jung, whose works lived in my bookshelves. I consulted his book, *Man and His Symbols*, for meaning. As a teenager, I'd rejected these internal mind movies, but I had become more accepting. *They are not logical, but they must be a window to my spirit. I just can't seem to crack the code and use them.* The visions haunted me. Time got away from me while I read and searched within. Before I realized it, my sessions for the day had ended and Jean was saying good night and wishing me a great weekend.

Standing inside of my closet was like coming face-to-face with my shopping addiction. Every impulse purchase and overpriced designer label stared back at me like a giant intervention. I was frozen from too many choices. I called Sandy for a second opinion.

"What do you think, businessy hoochie, conservative but fun? I have no idea how I want to look on this date," I said.

"Something tells me red, sexy, and powerful but feminine. What do you have in red?" she asked.

"I have a red dress with a teasing, swooped neckline. The fabric is clingy, and it has nice bell sleeves."

"That's it! Wear that. And let me know how it goes. Bye, bye, sweetie." Sandy hung up.

I pulled my brown dreadlocks into an updo, put on light makeup and false eyelashes that actually looked so real I had to wonder why I bothered, and added bronze frosty lipstick. I stepped into my clingy dress, proud of my size-8 curvy figure. I never wanted the waiflike, ten-year-old-boy look of those thin model types. I appreciated my curves, but I did have issues with my skin color. The dancing genetics in my mixed-race family landed just shy of a monochrome for me. If you blinked, my honey-brown skin, eyes, and hair all matched. I looked like a cartoon, an odd cute. The phone rang at the right time to interrupt my self-sabotage. Lance had called to say he was on the way over.

"I am in the car. I should be there in about five minutes," he said.

"OK, I'll keep an eye out for you." I hung up the phone and realized I hadn't asked if he would like to come up and see my place. Twenty minutes later, I watched from my condo window as this rattling BMW relic attempted to squeeze into a too-short parking space. I didn't expect the good-looking, successful doctor to drive what we used to call a hoop-dee car. It was old—not old like classic, old like ugly. I decided to keep an open mind and resisted the temptation to suggest that we take my car. Another piece of my fantasy about Lance had crumbled.

Let's see...clumsy, bad eyesight, had a date in front of me, talked about himself too much, and now a rattrap car. Why am I doing this?

I left the window to go downstairs and end Lance's parking pain.

He continued to move the car forward and backward without making progress. *I thought science and math were related brain gifts. Clearly, this spot is smaller than the car. He is so weird.*

"Hi there." I stood smiling and waving, waiting for his reaction to my red, tight-fitting but appropriate dress. I got the reaction I had hoped for as his eyes drew an obvious outline of my figure.

"You look fantastic." The compliment drained from his lips.

"Thank you. Let's roll." *If this piece of shit can roll.*

We soon approached Broadway and Twenty-Third Street. We found a lucky parking spot and walked into Sky.

"Sarah, would you like a cocktail while we wait for our table? We can take those two seats at the bar," Lance suggested.

"Great idea. I would love a vodka martini."

"Then we have something in common. I also prefer the vodka martini to gin. It is my favorite drink. I am partial to Grey Goose. What is your vodka of choice?" he asked.

"I like Grey Goose and Ketel One equally. I never developed a taste for scotch." I was rapidly growing tired of this conversation and started to fidget with the cocktail napkins. The fidgeting signaled that I was bored.

Bored before dinner, not a good sign. I need to move us into the direction of a more interesting conversation.

"Let me ask you my favorite icebreaker question," I said.

"Sure. Ask on." Lance smiled.

"What would you consider your most life-changing experience?"

Lance looked down. His expression turned serious.

"While shadowing a doctor during my premed studies, I saw him save a child's life. The child had gone into cardiac arrest. I will never forget the feeling of fear, excitement, and relief. It was powerful. I knew it was what I had to do and had to become." His voice carried a faint quiver. "I realized that I loved children in a committed way that I cannot totally explain. But I knew and know that I have to heal them." The revelation caused Lance to look down at the table, vulnerable and shy.

I placed my hand over his.

"That is incredible. Thank you for sharing that with me." I smiled.

As he spoke about his experience, I had forgotten all about the thick glasses, tasseled shoes, and the rattling car. I realized that I was attracted to something deeper. It was as if I could see beyond it all into the soul of this new man. The hostess interrupted, and we were led to a great table that presented a bit of privacy. Lance stood until I was seated. Within seconds, the waiter appeared.

"I bow to your expertise. Will you order for us?" Lance asked.

"Absolutely. We'll both start with the Sky magnolia salad. The gentleman will have sorghum-lacquered duck, and I will have the NOLA jambalaya risotto with no meat, please."

The waiter nodded and took our menus.

"I thought you were a vegetarian," Lance teased.

"I am, but I'm a fish-eating vegetarian. Truthfully, I can't make it through one week without seafood," I confessed.

He laughed. He had the laugh of the extremely bookish guys I had known. They laughed with a sucking-in sound that happened somewhere between the teeth, throat, and nose.

The restaurant had a nice hum of conversation, not too loud but lively. I stroked my martini glass because I was still a little nervous. But the conversation helped to calm me. It was no big surprise that my suspicions were correct and Lance's family had come to California from Louisiana in the 1950s, same as mine had.

"I made it a mission over the years to discard many of the negative superstitions and wives' tales so celebrated in the Louisiana culture. For example, I intentionally eat bananas at night." Lance attempted humor.

"Did your mama used to say that eating bananas at night would make you smother, too?" I asked.

"Oh, yes indeed. Even after I became a doctor and told her that was a wives' tale and not scientifically accurate, she still insisted." Lance laughed as if he had not laughed hard in a long time—again with the nerdy, suck-in, sniff sound. My attraction to him was on an emotional trapeze that swung from strong magnetism to boredom. It made sense if you knew Lance because he was an attractive doctor, a good catch. That part of him turned me on. The nerd that lived inside and peeled out in his laugh made me want to call it a night and keep moving. I decided to see it through.

I laughed with him and at him kindly. His care for his little patients had captured my heart.

"And to make it worse, I also eat red sauce made by women I did not know." Lance enjoyed his own humor and was on a roll with the Creole superstitions.

"Whoa, man!" I said.

I couldn't believe he knew about that disgusting spell. There was no need to say it because it was an old and well-known voodoo spell where a woman would put her menstruation blood into a red sauce to make a man fall in love with her. Anyone with Louisiana roots was familiar with it.

We spoke in clumsy unison, "A woman can put a spell on a man with red sauce!"

I guess we were louder than I thought because three Asian women sitting at the next table shot strange glances in our direction.

"That is dangerous territory. I hope no one really ever tried that," I said a bit more softly.

Lance's face turned serious.

"Although I have a French last name, when asked about it, I just say that my ancestors came from a plantation owned by the French."

That may have worked with people unfamiliar with Louisiana and its history, but I knew that Lance had a look that inferred more French involvement than simply work at the plantation. His mixed-race heritage was obvious.

"I choose to be Afrocentric." He was emphatic.

Apparently, Lance was one of the brothers who seemed to wish his skin were darker and his hair kinkier, but it hadn't happened that way for him. He had what some called the typical Louisiana look, very light, olive-yellow skin with black wavy hair. Like lighter-skinned Creoles, he looked Latino. And despite the black pride movement of the 1960s, the taboo issue of skin color and hair texture still plagued the African-American community.

"Do you resent the fact that some black folks still consider light skin superior?" I asked.

"Yes. I hate that. I hate that I look like I might believe that." He stated in a bit of anger.

"I understand. Some non-Creole African Americans think if you are light-skinned, you must think you are not black or are superior. And then, if you recognize your Creole culture, they think you want to be white or that you are ashamed of your African heritage. And the Creoles think you betray your roots when you don't acknowledge the culture. There's a lot of damned if you do and damned if you don't for us."

It felt good to share the common cultural baggage. Wearing dreadlocks was my way to embrace my African heritage, and it was possible that I was overcompensating in my own way. The common bond inspired my imagination. By the time dessert arrived, I was mentally planning our wedding. Lance never noticed that I was barely listening as he explained his college and medical school years in painful technicality and detail. I could feel the heat of attraction to the nerdy Adonis. Our drinks kept flowing, and soon, our knees touched under the table. He grabbed my hand and held it while he talked.

"At first, I could not make up my mind on a specialty," he droned on and on.

I smiled, ordered another martini, and wondered how the night would end.

Will he expect something? What do I do if he does? Hell, what do I do if he doesn't? Would he…no. Maybe yes. Oh my God, I sound like Corwin. Ah, shit!

The next morning ended the mystery. It was about 8:00 a.m. when I woke up and saw Lance in my bed. Blame it on the liquor, my tight dress, or the never-ending expectations; Lance got free milk this night, without buying the cow—as my mother often warned. And maybe, this time, she was right. This had not happened the way I would have wanted it to. It was too fast and just a blur. Lance and I were attracted to each other. Our hands touched frequently while we talked, and we even kissed a few times at the dinner table. But the rest of the night dissolved into a martini fog. We both had had too much to drink. It was like a night in Vegas, waking up with a stranger looking for your shoes. I couldn't remember most of it.

"Good, uh, morning," Lance gave an awkward greeting.

"Uh, yeah. Would you like some coffee or breakfast?" I had trouble sounding normal, even about cooking.

"No. Have to go. I have to get to the hospital. I will, uh, see you, uh, soon." He spoke in short phrases. The only thing worse than Lance's nerd-speak was his embarrassed nerd-speak.

He left my place so fast that his raggedy car must have left tire tracks in front of my building. And three days after our date, we still had not had a conversation. My phone rang a few times, but the caller would hang up as soon as I answered. One time, I didn't answer because it was my mom, and I wasn't up to talking to her after this. But the other calls were from Lance. I couldn't figure out why he didn't want to talk or why he failed to realize that caller ID nailed him even without a message. More than a week later, I heard his voice. Lance had left a voice message on my home phone late on a Thursday morning. It was a thinly veiled effort to avoid a conversation because he knew I'd be at my office.

Beep. "Sarah. Hi, it is, uh, Lance. I am really glad that we met. I enjoyed our dinner date; however, I just do not think we are quite right for each other. I have to say…" *Click!* I hung up.

I didn't listen to the rest of his long-winded kiss-off.

Verbose fucker!

It was time for me and the girls to dish on Lance, as he had now joined my long list of Mr. Wrongs. We decided to get together on a Thursday night. Nikeba wanted to talk about her upcoming anniversary party and wanted our help, so it was a good time to entertain the patrons at Night Jam's with our outrageous brand of girl talk. We met about 5:30 p.m. to eat sushi, drink, and dish.

I had the floor. "We do it all the time. We think a guy is great immediately, rather than get to know the real guy. We give them a hundred points and work down from there. I think they do the opposite. I think we start with zero and have to work up in their twisted minds. It's a stupid reflex action for me. I guess I really want a permanent partner in my life so bad that I dismiss any signs of flaws." I was pleading my case for fair and just dating.

"I used to do the same thing before meeting Raphael." Sandy was sympathetic. "I think we buy into thinking that a man can be more than human. They are just people, Sarah. Tempting as it is to imagine that magical prince, they are just people." She comforted me.

"Bullshit. Steve was not and is not perfect, but I never had that kind of trouble with him." Nikeba and her husband seemed to have had a particularly smooth dating experience.

"Well, in fairness, you guys met in high school. Did you really have a chance to experience grown-up dating issues? You two grew up together. It's not the same thing." I had to set the record straight.

"I don't buy it. A person is who they are, period. Chicken-shit is as chicken-shit does, at any age. Where is that waiter? Sarah, you will make me the closet alcoholic you are soon," Nikeba mumbled as she looked around to have her drink freshened.

"I am not an alcoholic. In my world, drinking is the norm. We drink. It's what we do. We don't get drunk often. But we drink often. It's one of the few things about my culture that I truly love," I stated in my defense.

"Latinos are the same," Sandy piped in. Sandy was a really white girl married to a really Latino man.

"Jews are the same. I got plowed at Steve's nephew's bar mitzvah." Nikeba snickered.

"The Irish are the same. To the Irish!" I raised my glass in a humorous toast.

"Don't forget the Italians." Sandy initiated another toast.

I looked down at my watch for no particular reason.

"How does this work, guys? When I'm too standoffish to make time to get to know them, it doesn't work. When I feel comfortable that I do know them, it doesn't work. You should have heard him talk about the way he loves kids and why he has to heal them. It was moving. I honestly felt that I was connecting to him," I whined a bit.

"There is no one simple answer to relationships. You remember the bad time I had dating Raphael. The closer we got, the more he'd run away. He would come close, run. Come close, and run again. It was frustrating," Sandy said.

"Yeah, but did he ever say you were not a match?" Nikeba asked, looking at Sandy.

"Yes, he did, Counselor. You don't remember, but he broke up with me several times," Sandy snapped a bit at Nikeba.

"That's right. Why are you married to him again?" Nikeba smiled and replaced the harsh tones in her voice with teasing.

"Well, even though I'm pissed and dissed, something tells me he is not a bad guy."

I couldn't explain the feeling and didn't bother to, but I felt Lance was still a good guy and my instincts told me that he and I were not over. Not yet.

"You and those feelings, visions, channeling, and voodoo—please come into the real world, Sarah. He fucked you and didn't call to say thanks. That spells jerk! Fuck him, but not literally this time," Nikeba insisted.

"Maybe you're right. And to make matters worse, it's time for that horrible family reunion of mine! Sorry that I'll miss your anniversary party this year. I have to go face the judgers in Louisiana. What's wrong with me?" I asked the rhetorical question because I was deep in thought and not really listening to my friends at that moment.

"Absolutely, nothing," Sandy insisted.

The three of us had a brief moment of unplanned silence and then moved into the discussion of Nikeba's anniversary party. We loved planning a good party, and the thought of it lifted the Lance cloud from over the table. While we talked, I couldn't help but wonder why it seemed so much easier for other women to have lasting relationships, especially for the women in my family.

Is there some secret handshake for the successful relationship club? And how in the world can I face Stacy at the reunion after a bad one-night stand? What is this reunion gonna be like now? Hell, maybe it's time for me to make red sauce.

My buzz had worn off quite a bit by the time I got home. It was only eight o'clock, so I decided that I'd better start packing for my early morning flight to Louisiana and to that Godforsaken reunion. I took great pains to pack outfits that had impressive designer labels. If I had to go to this damn reunion alone again and with a bruised ego, I might as well look successful.

While I packed, I glanced, once again, at the letter from Aunt Cat, my mother's sister. In it, she had shared family gossip and her premonitions as she had done in all of her letters over the years. This letter was in Aunt Cat's typical vision code.

The last paragraph read, "I hate to say, but get ready to handle a very bad time, mon chér, and den comes a very good time. Dat don't mean today. Just mean it's a-comin'. With much love, Nyés Sarah. T tante, Cat."

As usual, I had no idea what the hell that meant. Little did Aunt Cat know, I had just had a very bad time, and now, I had to face the family, which meant a worse time was definitely a-comin'.

CHAPTER THREE

I rarely set my alarm clock, but in order to be ready at 4:00 a.m. I decided it would be best. It screamed. I obeyed and was ready to go within half an hour. Surprisingly, it still wasn't too early for my long-suffering mother, known as Ma-ma, to pester me. She was already in Louisiana, and the time zone had given her two hours on me. She used them.

The phone rang.

"Just checking on you, Sarah. You said your flight was at seven. Just wanted to make sure you didn't miss it." Her voice was always stern. It was her style.

"No, Ma-ma, I'm on time. I finished with my packing last night, and I'm waiting for the shuttle." I implied *so get off of the phone*, but she ignored it.

"Well, I wish you had flown with the rest of us; it would have been so easy to work out. Guess you were out drinking with your friends again. We got in last night, and we're having a pleasant morning here." She always made statements sound like orders.

I had lied about having something I had to do so that I could avoid traveling with my recently widowed Ma-ma; my brother, Lyle, and his wife, Tracy, and their kids, Drew and Dawn. Also in the party was my difficult sister, Lizette, with her beaten-down husband, Tom, and their daughter, Riley.

My brother and sister lived lives as orderly and conformist as the alliteration in their names. The highlight of these forced-fit family gatherings was Aunt Cat. Her stories of family scandal and mysterious events seemed to bring the past dramatically back to life. She took the boredom out of these events. It was no secret that I was her favorite and the only one who had inherited the gift of visions.

The family reunion was being held outside of Lafayette in an unincorporated area close to the town of Franklin. The area was a south Louisiana mecca of great food, thick Creole French accents, and the celebration of alcoholic beverages. Where else in the world could you buy daiquiris at drive-through locations?

It was still dark outside two hours before flight time when I climbed into a shuttle for the Oakland airport, holding a first-class ticket and a bad attitude. To make things worse, I saw Corwin trying to hide behind a streetlight on the corner while I was adjusting my seat belt. It took my breath away. I had had underlying concern for Corwin's wife and family, fearing that he could potentially snap and harm them. I wasn't convinced it would happen, but I knew it was possible. For the first time, however, I felt that *I* should also be wary of Corwin. His stalking was escalating. I was doing my best to bring him to functionality within the so-called societal norms, but I wasn't seeing the results I had hoped to see. True to form, he was wearing a bowler this time to keep his head protected from his bad spirits.

Does he really think that I can't see him? What's disturbing is he's outside of my home at this hour. I will deal with him as soon as I get back.

Leaving the Corwin issue until I returned, I had a little fun mentally rehearsing answers to the predictable and anticipated questions from family about dates and relationships that I would have to navigate.

Stacy: Well, Sarah, you came alone—again?

Me: Yes, Stacy. I meet better men than you ever will in this dirt-water town, so they are really busy and…it's a bit harder to marry them.

Stacy: How would you know anything about marrying a man? You don't have a track record, chér.

Me: Oh. Do you call what you do marriage? Why don't you just set a day rate?

I would love to have that much fun with that insufferable witch.

We arrived at the airport within twenty minutes. I tipped the shuttle driver and was boarding the plane in record time. The nearly six-hour flight with a plane change was enough time to organize the lies and make up a boyfriend who was too busy to attend. I planned to use Lance as the busy boyfriend and not the rat he actually had turned out to be. Changing planes in Houston reminded me of long-winded Lance as he talked about his undergraduate years at Rice University. I felt a sense of sadness and then chased the thought away with a drink and a nap. The flight attendant woke me up for landing.

"Miss? Miss, we are getting ready to land and you need to pull your seat to its upright position."

As I got off the plane, the thick, humid Louisiana air filled my nose and made my breathing labored. Lafayette had not changed much over the past two years since my last visit. Its oil boom and bust made for a small, moderately active airport that was easy to navigate. I was in a rental car in no time. As I began driving east on Highway 90 out of Lafayette to the rural area where my family waited, my mind was preoccupied with getting through the next few days with as little emotional pain as possible. I could kill Lance for breaking my heart before this high-pressure event. Before I could complete that thought, my cell phone rang.

"Dr. Sarah? It's Jean."

"Yeah, Jean?"

"How was your flight?" she asked.

"Just fine. I'm leaving the airport but have a little driving to do. What's going on?" I asked.

"Just to let you know, Mr. Corwin was taken to the hospital today. I got a call from his wife. She said it wasn't a suicide attempt this time. He fainted just before ten o'clock this morning. She wanted you to know."

"Well, that's better than his usual. You know the drill. Make sure we get a copy of his chart to the hospital, so they have a clear record of his mental state and medications."

I was almost matter-of-fact because Corwin regularly had drama in his life. I chose not to tell Jean he was outside of my building earlier that morning. I didn't want her to worry. I had decided not to take action against him. He was his own worst enemy.

"And why are you at the office, Jean? It's Friday, and I'm not there. Go home," I insisted.

"It's a good time for me to catch up on some paperwork and orga-nize some files. I'll leave early. I promise!" Jean chuckled.

She wished me a good trip and hung up. After an hour's drive down the lonely highway, I approached the long driveway and private road of what we still referred to as "Gramp's house." It was next door to my wonderful aunt Cat's home. I could hear my tires crackle against the small white clamshells used to pave the driveway, another signature of rural Louisiana. Branches of the oak trees in Gramp's large front yard hung heavy with Spanish moss, which gave them a haunting beauty. Gramp's house had been the family's summer gathering place before he passed away and remained the center of our activities. I stretched as I got out of the car, and Aunt Cat walked toward me. I spoke very little Creole French but always made the effort out of respect.

"Konmen ça va, Tante?" (How are you, Auntie?)

"Bien, et toi, Sarah?" (I am fine and you, Sarah?)

Aunt Cat was a very petite woman with Indian copper-tinged skin. Her long, straight nose; high cheekbones; and kitten-soft straight hair were an exact duplicate of my mother's, but with an additional nineteen years. She stood four feet five inches with a ninety-five-pound frame. Her hands and feet would seem childlike except for the exposed veins of age. Aunt Cat was in her nineties, but she could easily have passed for a woman sixty-five or seventy.

"It's so good to see ya, yeah, Sarah."

"Oh, Auntie, I am so glad to see you, too." Aunt Cat was really more my mother than Ma-ma. We seemed to share one spirit and got along well. Ma-ma and I rarely agreed upon anything. Aunt Cat was the family griot or oral historian with decades of family history stored in her memory. She shared the stories in order to keep them alive. She spoke melodically in English interspersed with Creole French. She also sometimes used gris-gris bags or voodoo dolls for what she called positive spells, but she preferred to light colored candles in order to exact justice or to use chants for blessings and herbs and roots for healing. Aunt Cat used black candles for protection, green candles for money, blue for luck, and white to ask for justice against an offender.

"Come bring you bags in da house and sit with us on da porch, chér." Aunt Cat returned to her spot on the porch.

Steam was coming from huge black cast-iron kettles on the front lawn. They were filled with spices, crabs, crawfish, corn, and potatoes. It looked as if about twenty of my relations—men, women, and children—had gathered this year for the reunion at Gramp's. The adults sat in the large front yard talking, drinking, and playing cards while the children played on the oak tree swings.

But the pleasant mood was not to last. It seemed all birds and animals began to scatter as a sign that something wicked was nearby. Animals didn't really run from Stacy, but they should have. She and her henpecked husband, number whatever, drove up and got out of the car. Stacy was Aunt Cat's daughter, but didn't share her gift of visions or good heart.

"Sarah, chér, how you doin', my couzan?" She came right for me, arms extended.

"I'm fine, Stacy. How have you been?" I gave her a distant hug.

"Oh, you look so good and prosperous." Stacy looked me up and down. She always gave other women a total body review to size up the competition. Every woman was competition to Stacy.

"Did you bring a man with you this trip? You independent women, I don't know how you manage without a husband. I couldn't imagine not having Robert." Stacy smiled the smile of the evil.

"I couldn't imagine you without Robert either, Stacy." I smiled back, biting my tongue and the insides of my cheeks.

Stacy and I had a history of public arguments, and I regret to say, at least one hair-pulling catfight at a wedding. She had pushed my buttons, so I pushed her face into a dessert tray.

"Well, if you are in the market, Robert and me know of a really nice bachelor who moved to town last month. He is working on some type of fellowship or research grant in geology and came here to study the soil in this area. Can we introduce you? He's been to dinner with us a couple of times, and he never brings a woman." Stacy tried to embarrass me and, unfortunately, had succeeded.

31

"Stacy, I am seeing someone." I let it out with conviction and made it sound true.

"Oh, you *have* a man this time. Is he coming?" she spit the question out with a pinch of doubt.

Snide bitch.

"No, he's a doctor and couldn't get away." The back of my neck boiled with the heat of anger and shame.

Stacy was one of those women who wore her marriages and husbands like a social badge of honor. She was on her third husband. The first husband divorced her because he caught her with another man. The second husband was the other man, and the third was Robert, a mouse. Stacy also had a weird habit of wearing all of her old wedding and engagement rings. Her right hand was a monument to former lovers. She adored jewelry and wore it with jogging outfits as her signature casual look. On this day, she was wearing her favorite color, pink, and despite her horrible personality, she was an extraordinarily attractive woman. She had huge breasts, a small waist, and generous hips. Her wavy, shoulder-length hair was jet-black, shiny, and framed her olive-colored face. Her eyes were large, deep-brown almonds, and she had the nose and cheekbones of both our mothers. Her lips were full and perfectly shaped. Most men licked their lips when they saw Stacy.

"Yes, I do *have a man.* Lance is on call at the hospital this weekend," I said.

"Oh, well, just let us know." Stacy backed down. She had already won.

I could sense that the rest of the family members had turned their attentions away from Stacy and me. I was humiliated and trumped again by this uneducated shrew. I held a plastered smile on my face and climbed three steps to enter the screened porch when I met my mother's pitying eyes.

"Don't worry, Sarah," my mother tried to comfort me. She struggled to hide her embarrassment. She held her right hand to her cheek in her sign of concern.

"You didn't tell me you were dating a doctor? Is that true? If it's not true, don't worry, chér. I keep telling you, it'll happen for you when you least expect it. You don't have to make up a man to impress Stacy," Ma-ma offered.

I was her disappointment, the daughter who couldn't get a husband or even a steady boyfriend. She had spent fifty years with one man, my father. He wouldn't let her work outside of our home, drive a car, or cut her hair, so I couldn't bear to listen to man advice from my mom. We had nothing in common.

"Ma-ma, I'm not making it up. I met a doctor, and it's still pretty new so I didn't want to say anything yet. I just get tired of everybody harping on the fact that I'm single. I'm single. I am single, OK. What is the big deal? Do we not allow single people to remain in the family?" I asked loudly.

"I was just trying to make you feel better. You looked a little down after Stacy made her remarks. Don't pay attention to her. But she does have a way with men…"

"Please, Ma, I don't want to talk about Stacy's way with men," I snapped.

"Bernice, leave her be about a man. I wish my daughter would stop marrying so damn many men." Aunt Cat was visibly irritated. "Sarah will be fine. Now, leave her alone." Aunt Cat had, once again, come to my rescue.

"I just pray that things will work out for you. I just don't want you to be alone in life." My mother ended with that statement, stood up, and walked into the house, leaving the screen door to screech as it swung closed.

I found myself fighting back tears.

I am probably wealthier than anyone here. Why do I always feel sorry for myself when I'm around these people? I guess it's because I know they all feel sorry for me.

I carried my Louis Vuitton bags, those thoughts, and a heavy heart into the house. I knew which room. It was the equivalent of the kids' table at Thanksgiving and a familiar spot because the other rooms had to accommodate couples. I found my way to the room set up for the kids and the unmarried past age twenty-five or…me. I put my bags between two rollaway beds. Tired from the long flight and

33

eager to be alone, I changed into a robe and took a nap that lasted into the next morning. I knew that the stage had now been set for this reunion. As I gave in to my drowsiness, I started to go over my latest visions, especially the disturbing one with blood on a wedding dress. I wondered if there was a Stacy connection. Was I really getting married or in danger? I just couldn't get complete pictures in my visions.

The sun made warm lace-curtain images on my face, and I blinked a few times to wake up. My dreams didn't provide any particular insight. My kiddie roommates were already up and outside playing, so I used the time to hang my things in the large black-painted armoire. I had slept through the night without first unpacking. Through the opened window, I heard some of my cousins calling me. The loudest voice belonged to Vereen, Stacy's more likeable sister. I lifted the window and poked my head out of it.

"Sarah, you know we gotta go out later tonight. You up for Le Bon Temps? What if we leave at about nine? Is that OK?" Vereen was yelling from her car. She lived about three miles down the rural road in a modest home with her husband and three children. She was in her minivan.

"That sounds like a plan, Vereen."

"I have to run some errands, but I'll be back later. Most people are gonna go their own way during the day today, so I won't be back till tonight," she yelled.

Vereen had a great husband. He was soft-spoken and a good guy who could be fun. But she seemed to do all of the heavy-lifting in their marriage. She rarely complained, but when she did need to let off some steam, she talked to me.

I wasn't in the mood to socialize with Stacy and that tree stump husband of hers, but I knew they would be part of the gang. I put my hurt feelings aside and accepted my role as fifth wheel.

"I'll be ready!" I yelled back.

I waved bye to Vereen and put my head back inside of the window. The large mantel clock on the bedroom fireplace gonged ten o'clock.

A swoosh of color hit my forehead with a sharp pain. Another vision. I saw myself picking up a man from an airport. It was in Oakland, and for the first time, I could feel emotion. I was happy. I was really happy. This vision was a minor breakthrough. I thought it meant a man would visit. *Who? Hell, who cares? It's progress.* I couldn't see the man's face. I stood still and waited for the pain in my head to leave. I pulled myself together quickly, putting on a pair of jeans, a sage-green tank top, and sage-green sandals. I pulled my locks into a ponytail and went into the kitchen. Ma-ma and Aunt Cat were sitting at the round oak table sharing stories over strong chicory coffee.

"There's my girl. How did you sleep?" Ma-ma was cheerful.

"I slept longer than I expected; guess I was pretty tired," I answered.

"I heard Vereen call ya. I'm glad you young people are gonna have some fun. How many goin'?" Aunt Cat asked.

"I'm not sure, Aunt Cat, but I guess we'll take Vereen's van. If we need my rental car, I can drive, too."

"If you will be drinking, maybe you shouldn't. You're not used to these roads. There are hardly any lights and—"

I held my hand up in a rude halt.

"Ma-ma. Just stop," I ordered.

"Sarah, I'm just concerned with drinking and driving," she said.

"Ma-ma, you are concerned with air and water. Everything gives you concern and a reason to fly a dark cloud over everything. Maybe everything will be fine. Maybe we won't have the car crash that ends our lives. Maybe we will just have fun!" I didn't plan to shout at my mom, but it came out.

"All right, don't mark da day with bad spirits. Both of ya, shut up. Look at God's sky and be glad ya can see it. Be glad ya got health and money. Stop all dat damn arga-in'." Aunt Cat's eyes were narrow with irritation.

Aunt Cat pronounced words in her unique way and "arga" was one of them. It was her way of saying "argue," but we knew what she meant. We also knew she rarely raised her voice, so we both shut up.

"You know Lizette and Lyle took their families to the hotel in Franklin. They said no need to cram up so much since some of the others had gotten here first this year with kids and all." Ma-ma strained to make conversation.

"That makes sense. I fell asleep so fast, I wondered where they were." I played along.

"They're visiting a few people and will come in around four or five o'clock. Catin, when do you want dinner served?" Ma-ma often used Aunt Cat's full name, which was Catin with a French pronunciation.

"Well, let's say we have it all ready 'round five?" Aunt Cat replied.

"I told Stacy what to start on dis mornin', and she'll be here in a few minutes."

Stacy was now chief cook since Aunt Cat was older and preferred to supervise.

I knew that every Louisiana meal began with the Holy Trinity of onions, bell pepper, and celery, so I offered to begin cutting up herbs for seasoning.

"Aunt Cat, how about I start chopping the seasoning?"

"Dat sounds good, Sarah."

"I'll help her." Ma-ma sounded like an eager child.

"No, ma'am. You come with me outside. You can help me get dis yard together, and we can gossip some more." The sisters chuckled and went outside.

Within the hour, the screen door screeched as I heard Stacy call my name.

"Sarah. Sarah? Are you here? I'm gonna start the meats and bigger dishes," she said.

I had already cut and refrigerated the herbs.

"Oh, I need some personal things from the store. I cut up a ton of seasoning for you and put them in the refrigerator. See ya when I get back," I said, going for my car keys and rushing out.

I got into the car and then wondered what I would buy. Who cared? I would avoid spending time alone in the kitchen with Stacy. Worked for me.

I returned a little shy of five o'clock. The crowd had formed in the front yard, and our procession of dishes had begun. The men had set up several tables according to Aunt Cat's instructions: one served as a buffet, one for a bar, and several others for eating and card games of bid whist and dominoes.

Potato salad, fried fish, boiled shrimp, and an assortment of vegetables later, we were all stuffed—but never too stuffed for pies and cakes. The men pulled out Grand Marnier and Jack Daniel's to lace our coffees. Vereen tapped my arm playfully.

"Don't get too sleepy. We gotta go to Le Bon Temps. We're gonna go home and change. We'll let the kids stay here with the other children. We'll be back."

This was a big night for Vereen. It was one of the few times she was able to go out and have a good time. I helped the other women to clean up the yard and take food inside before going to my quarters to change clothes. I picked out a pair of tan pants and a cream-colored, lightweight sweater. I accessorized with a gold belt, gold flat shoes, and emerald costume jewelry. I had just finished a quickie shower and dressing when Vereen honked the horn of her van.

"Come on, old folks! It's late! Let's go while we can still get tables!" Vereen yelled to rush us up. She was parked in the long driveway between Gramp's and Aunt Cat's houses. Our cousins started filing out of both houses, and we loaded up like schoolkids into the van and one car. Despite my protests to Ma-ma, I decided not to drive. Vereen was used to driving the dark country highways of Franklin to Le Bon Temps. Twenty minutes and an impromptu singalong of old Motown songs on the radio later, the caravan of Jean-Louis relations pulled into the concrete, moon-surface parking lot of Le Bon Temps.

"I'm glad I wore flat shoes. Will they ever fix the concrete of this parking lot?" I was irritated.

"Well, you know us in the country. We don't care so much about rough parking lots." Stacy used her bittersweet voice.

"Stacy, we don't like it either; the Francis family just won't do anything about it." With that, Vereen stopped a further Sarah-Stacy match.

The Francis family owned Le Bon Temps, and nearly all of the men in that family worked at the club. We walked in, and the unique sounds and smells of a real Louisiana juke joint greeted us at the door.

We heard an R&B song end, and a Zydeco tune began in Creole patois, wailing about love and life. I looked down at the familiar knotty wood floors and thought how absolutely different this club was from Marlin on the Bay in Berkeley. My eyes scanned the walls to see if anything had changed since my last time there, but it hadn't.

"Wow. That Jax beer neon sign still has a blinking A," I mused.

"Yeah, things don't change much!" Vereen laughed.

Two out-of-date, grease-stained insurance company calendars were held in place with tacks above the worn wood-topped bar that was trimmed in metal. I took a deep breath and savored the smell of hot links, seasoned fried shrimp, and French fries that cooked in the backroom kitchen.

Le Bon Temps was dark, even in daylight. All eyes stared as the big group of Jean-Louises searched for a table. We were gossip fodder in town, like most well-respected families. We found an area, and the waiter helped us move three limping tables together. Seated, I decided to start a conversation, so I picked on Stacy's Robert.

"Robert, it is really amazing that over the past twenty years, this place has not changed much at all." That comment seemed benign.

"Yeah, this place will stay this way forever." Robert smiled the smile of the dense. It was as if there was a hollow behind his eyes and between his ears. His mouth opened to reveal teeth that didn't all face in the same direction. And his eyes seemed linked to a brain without thoughts.

"Do people still come here to creep out on their spouses?" I teased.

"Oh, let's not bring up all that..." Stacy was irritated. Guess that remark struck too close to home for her.

"Shit, people still come here to cheat. It's the low lights," Vereen answered.

The other cousins started side conversations, and thankfully, our waiter had come to get our orders.

"OK, that's three rum and Cokes, two Jack and sevens, a scotch rocks, two beers, and a vodka martini." The waiter repeated our orders. I, of course, was the martini. My heart stung with the memory of my last martini with Lance. I dismissed the thought before Stacy or anyone else could pick up on the sadness of that memory.

My cousin Trey, who had come in from Maryland, pointed to Mr. Thibodeaux, who was dancing alone. It made me think of the vision I had of myself dancing alone. Thibodeaux was a drunken fixture, much like the mix-matched furniture of Le Bon Temps.

"Aren't you a bit jealous of his bliss?" I asked.

"Hell, after a few drinks, we'll all be that blissful!" Robert beamed.

Whoa. Robert actually said something funny.

I got my drink and sipped gratefully as I continued to people-watch. I closed my eyes and noticed how the smell of earth competed with the aroma of smoke and liquor. Many of the people worked on farms or at the local sugar-cane mill, and coming to Le Bon Temps was a big night out for them.

I felt someone looking at me. I turned around and saw a man who seemed out of place at the club. It's a funny thing in small towns, you can always tell the visitors. It could be the style and fit of their clothes, the gait, an attitude—all of it. He smiled. I saw a perfect chocolate face with beautiful white teeth framed with a thin moustache. He smiled broadly. No glasses. He was impeccably dressed in (my guess) an Armani maroon sweater, tassel-less Italian loafers, and deep gray slacks. His face had the chiseled symmetry and square jaw of a male model. I fought my attraction to him. I reluctantly smiled back. I wasn't ready to meet anyone, and I sure as hell didn't want to meet anyone while in rural Louisiana. I was out for a drink, a dance, and to get the whole reunion thing over with, but he walked over.

"Hi. Would you like to dance?"

"No. But thank you." I barely looked at him.

"Oh. I'll check with you later." He walked away.

About two songs later, I felt a tap on the shoulder. I was about to become irritated and offer my go-away-dog look, but I was tickled when I turned around.

"Woul…would shjoo like to…da…dans…pretty gurl?"

Oh no, not drunken Thibodeaux!

"No. But thanks, Mr. Thibodeaux."

"Das OK, OK. I gon' dansh me." Thibodeaux swayed and slurred off. He resumed his solo performance.

"Boy, you are attracting all the men tonight." Stacy capitalized on the moment.

"Yeah, I'm pure gold." I flashed a big, insincere grin.

But Stacy's ridicule made me do what I had not planned to do and that was to accept the second offer from the attractive stranger.

"Are you ready to bust a move?"

I nodded and joined him on the dance floor. At least the song was a fast one and I didn't have to hug the stranger or talk to him. Despite that, he leaned in to talk to me over the music.

"Where are you visiting from? You obviously don't live here." He smiled broadly, and the ice was broken.

This guy was slick and smooth. My instincts told me he was trouble, but boy, he had come in a fine package. He had sparkling eyes and that flirty expression that seemed to have a permanent place on his face. He struck me as a mischievous guy. He was a Taye Diggs–type.

"My name is Michael Rousseau. I'm in town visiting my relatives for a few days." He continued to try to pull a conversation out of me.

He didn't have a local accent. And he was gorgeous enough to make Stacy visibly jealous, a bonus for me.

"My name is Sarah Jean-Louis. We're all in town for a family reunion."

When the song ended, I motioned for the table, and Michael escorted me to my seat. He sat next to me in one of the rockier chairs. I didn't bother to introduce everyone because half of my group was on the dance floor, dancing badly.

"Some of our group is on the dance floor," I said and pointed to them.

Michael looked at my cousins and raised his eyebrows in amused judgment.

We held a superficial conversation about Louisiana and Le Bon Temps. He had not visited much when he was a child but was beginning to see his aging relatives more often now.

"If I promise that I won't talk much, can I sit here a little longer and visit with you and your family?" Michael pretended to beg and let his limping chair roll in my direction.

"Well, it's kind of just family." My gut instincts were at war with my post-Lance stinging heart.

"Or can I just sit here and talk to myself…just sitting at your table? Just sitting. Talking to myself. Just me." Michael drummed his fingers on the table and flashed a brilliant smile.

I was now smiling, too. "Well, OK, but we're not going to have fun. No fun allowed." I was ready to play a little.

Michael gave an overstated thank-you. He watched the dance floor and did not talk at all for the first few minutes. As the cousins returned to the table, they all introduced themselves. Stacy was not very skilled in hiding envy.

"Glad to meet you. I'm Sarah's cousin Stacy." Her smile was tight, and her large eyes had turned into slits of resentment.

Michael nodded.

I turned to Michael, but before I could speak, a bright-blue flash rocked my forehead and caused me to tilt a bit in my chair. A brief vision had played in front of my head. I saw a man riding in my car in Oakland. I was driving the car, and he turned to me and opened his mouth to say something, but the vision faded before he spoke.

"I'm sorry, I sometimes get dizzy. It will pass."

That was all I chose to share with the stranger and the relatives. I excused myself and went into the tiny bathroom. I wanted to put something cold on my face, but the smell of concrete and old urine inspired me to pass on that idea. This was the longest vision I had ever had. And it played out in much more detail. Finally! I could link two visions and predict my future! Michael must be the guy riding in my car from the Oakland airport! This was huge for me. I was more excited about the vision than about Michael. And as I think back on it, these clues were a large part of the reason I let my guard down with Michael prematurely. I later learned that just because I saw something via my spirit gifts, it didn't necessarily mean it was a good thing. I washed my hands and rejoined my table.

41

"Are you OK? You used to hold your liquor better, ti Sarah." Stacy didn't miss a shot at trying to embarrass me.

"I'm good. I think it's the heat." I refused to engage Stacy's bait in front of Michael. I turned my attention back to him.

"Michael, where are you visiting from?" I was fueled by Stacy's jealousy and played with my left earring, flirty. Michael perked up at my attention to him. His smile grew.

"Um, Phoenix. I live in Phoenix. My aunt and uncle live here, but most of our family is in New Iberia and Lafayette, up the road, as they say," he explained.

"I live in Oakland. I grew up in Berkeley, and our family is mainly in Franklin and all over the US," I said.

For the next hour or so, Michael and I talked. The rest of the group seemed to disappear, and were it not for the music, even the club would have become distant. I was happy to feel the attention of another man so soon after being rejected. This was the time when I usually would spill my guts in one long, run-on sentence about everything. But I decided to take my own counsel, and I broke that pattern. I summarized my life and my eventual decision to become a therapist with no personal or emotional overload.

"I was fascinated with family therapy. I thought that if I could open my own office, I could practice my way. I have my own approach to healing family relationships and treatment." I sensed that I was going on too long, but I couldn't hide my enthusiasm.

"What do you do?" I asked before I started gushing.

"I'm an engineer. I didn't really know what an engineer did when I was growing up, but I was so good at science and math that one of my high school teachers thought I should consider mechanical engineering as a major. *Fascinated* is too strong a word for me, but I'm pretty charged up when I make things happen at the refinery. It's like a giant Erector Set for me." Michael showed his straight and nearly perfect white teeth.

"You know, now that we're talking, I can share with you a coincidence. I always wanted to live in California, so I recently jumped at the opportunity to apply for a job at ARCO in Los Angeles. I have been a frequent visitor to California and hope to be moving there," he said.

"Good luck with that." *Oh, yes! My vision is on point!*

It was nearly midnight when Vereen asked if we all were ready to leave. I was tired and politely told Michael good night as my group stood up.

"Can I see you again?" Michael asked.

"I don't know if that really makes sense." I played it cautious.

"Hey, what's wrong with a new friend, especially a new friend who might be moving to LA?" he joked.

"Well, OK. Here's my cell phone number."

I wrote it on one of the less-soaked cocktail napkins. I then joined my group as they walked back onto the moon-surface parking lot toward Vereen's van and the other car. I did notice that Michael stayed inside of the club and didn't walk me out to say good night—not that I wanted a hasty connection, but I thought back to something Nikeba would always say about men. She said men show you who they are when you first meet them by their manners and attentiveness or lack thereof. And it's important not to ignore the signs. Sandy, on the other hand, compared men to blind insects: no real plan, just bumping into what comes along until something sticks.

Do I want him to stick? He probably won't call. But there was that vision.

CHAPTER FOUR

"**T**here is always a damn rooster somewhere when I come here." Gramp's chicken coop had long been closed down, but there was one somewhere. And it was much too early for man, woman, or the little colorful beast to be awake, but it crowed. I got up and mastered the rollaway beds obstacle course to make it to the bathroom. The smell of coffee with chicory and Louisiana spices was an aroma that could not be duplicated anywhere in the world. I had a quick shower, put on some prewashed jeans with a torn-but-chic T-shirt, and pulled my dreadlocks into a ponytail holder. I went for the coffee and the food.

Our tradition was an early Sunday breakfast that crawled into a lazy lunch that slid into the main reunion dinner, and we would be joined by any latecomers at that point. After the reunion dinner, we would all scatter with lightning speed to return to our daily lives. Some left Sunday night and others Monday or Tuesday. Our reunions revolved around partying, food, cards, gossip, and sometimes a *boucherie* or *cochon de lait*, where the men roasted a pig, not the traditional reunion packages with T-shirts or cruises. One year, there was fishing, but that didn't last very long because of potential danger for the children. We owned a levee to the bayou behind Gramp's house, but the water had an eerie quality and was very deep, so we kept our festivities on dry land. There had been several drownings in that part of the bayou over the years. We liked the reunions less formal and more about getting together than a fully planned agenda. My mother and Aunt Cat were the grande dames and organizers of the reunion now, which meant they set the date and contacted everyone. The two of them were sitting at the round antique oak kitchen table drinking coffee while Stacy, Vereen, and two other cousins worked culinary magic.

"Can I help?" I bounced in.

"No, chér, we got it. Get yourself some coffee. We made some egg 'n' shrimp."

Stacy was an incredible cook. I hated that. This was another competitive area between us. I looked into the serving dish and saw picture-perfect fluffy scrambled eggs with a side of cheese sauce laced with shrimp and green onions. The toast was made from homemade bread, and the smell of yeast was seductive. They were all meat eaters and had a separate dish of bacon, sausage, and pork chops. That part of the breakfast was not tempting for me as the lone vegetarian, but the rest was mouthwatering. I noticed that the men and children had gathered in the front yard and waited to be served. I bowed to the spirit of Gramp for turning even the visiting men into Creole chauvinists. I grabbed coffee and helped out before filling my plate. Stacy and I took on the role of waitstaff for everyone. Ma-ma and Aunt Cat had moved to the tables outside. Sadly, the pleasant moment wouldn't last.

"You met a nice-looking man last night, yeah, couzan? What will you do now about what's-his-name?" Stacy held a large tray of scrambled eggs and cheese sauce and managed to fill plates while serving up her nice-nasty remarks.

"Oh, Stacy, I'm not looking to marry every man I meet. Michael could make a good friend." I used long tongs to serve up the sacrificed animals and was tempted to use them to pinch Stacy's large ass.

Stacy didn't miss my verbal slap and gave one back. "Maybe you should be lookin' to marry because you know your clock has passed, chér."

"I can't think that way in my situation. With my business as successful as it is, I stand to lose a lot more than I would gain in a hasty marriage."

That remark was beneath me, but I couldn't resist hitting her in the modest finances. In a move that was so surprising it should have come with its own gasp, Stacy's husband, Robert, spoke up. His voice was deep with intention but small from his...smallness.

"Stacy, stop commenting on Sarah's life. We're all sick of it. Everybody's different."

Not exactly profound, but at least he had tried.

I never disliked Robert; I just felt he had the presence of a hologram. It was easy to ignore the short, stodgy, medium-brown-skinned man. His wavy hair was cowlicked, and he was beginning to show the early signs of a beer belly. With my love of clothes, I cringed at the sight of his outfits. He wore black nylon socks with dress shoes, plaid shorts, and a Hawaiian shirt.

But he had defended me, so I just smiled at his classic tourist attire.

It was obvious that Michael's attraction to me had Stacy boiling with jealousy. She always wanted to be the most attractive woman in the room. Maybe Robert was finally growing tired of her miserable personality. My analysis was that Robert had an extreme aversion to confrontation, supported by his lack of balls. One manifestation of this was his tendency to quickly redirect awkward moments using non sequiturs. I considered it a classic sign of avoidance. After chastising Stacy, he used one of his coping devices.

"You know, researchers now say that real butter is healthier than all of these margarines?"

Robert buttered his bread liberally as he cowered. In a kind and generous move, another one of the men picked up on the theme of *foods once considered bad* and gave life to the meaningless discussion that evolved into a predictable man contest. When my brother, Lyle, chimed in, I thought to myself that the testosterone-laden pompous-ass discussions were now in session. As the men impressed each other with their knowledge of useless facts, Stacy and I seemed to call a silent truce, knowing we were both about to go too far. The next couple of hours moved slowly. It was time to clean up, so I balanced dishes and worked my way into the kitchen. I filled the sink with water and dishwashing liquid. I decided to be the designated dishwasher since that type of machine did not exist in Gramp's kitchen.

"Oh, you don't have to do those all by yourself." Stacy offered to stay and help.

"Oh no, it's not a problem for me. You said that you wanted to go home and then come back for dinner, so I'll do this." I had again avoided spending one-on-one time with Stacy.

"OK then. See you later, chér." I watched as Stacy touched the arm of her husband. His head bobbed up and down with drowsiness. The two of them left.

I began my work at the farm-style kitchen sink. I loved the red-and-white curtains that stood in place of cabinets beneath the sink. My cell phone was nearby, and I had convinced myself I needed it near in case a patient or Jean called me. But in my heart of hearts, I was waiting for a call from Michael. By the time I dried the last pot, my cell phone rang. I lunged for the phone and then turned around to see if anyone had witnessed that. It was him.

"Hello, lady. Did I really meet you last night, or was that a dream?" Michael flirted.

"Did you really use that line on me, or is this just a nightmare?" I shot back.

"Fair enough, I thought it would be funny, but it didn't work, did it?"

"Nope, it didn't." I chuckled.

"I am happy that we met, and I'd like to see you before I leave. I'll be flying back to Phoenix tomorrow morning. I know you guys have your reunion, but do you have any time today?"

The sincerity had returned to Michael's voice. I was hesitant but curious and wanted to see him now, too. My commitment to break old patterns inspired me to avoid inviting Michael to the actual family event because it would seem overly eager and too much, too soon. Plus, if my vision was accurate, I needed to pace myself. According to the vision, I could expect him to visit me in the Bay Area and our relationship to begin.

"It is our family dinner, but you could come around seven o'clock for coffee and dessert. That could work," I said.

"You got it. I'll be there at seven. I'll see you for dessert."

I gave him directions, and he hung up.

While I wiped off the table and stove, I wondered what kind of impression Michael would make. I thought back to the last time I had introduced the family to a love interest. I was in graduate school, and I brought my then-boyfriend to the reunion that year. He hit on two of my cousins, including Stacy, further inflating her ego. I had to ask him to leave. It was humiliating. I remember Ma-ma kept her hand on her right cheek, her sign of embarrassment and concern, for several hours that day. Because Ma-ma lived through us, my degradation was her degradation. I smiled to myself. These things were always funnier looking back. I finished cleaning the kitchen and returned to the bedroom. I grabbed a moment with the hot quiet breezes coming into the window for a nap. It was about three when I woke up and tuned in to the sounds of people laughing and talking. I had slept through lunch. I had an abstract dream. In it, I was walking down a long hallway with no windows and no doors. Again, I could identify my emotions. I felt absolute terror. I could feel myself shaking when I got up. I didn't have my books to research the symbols, but my visions and dreams seemed to have meanings of their own. Not even Carl Jung could decipher these for me. I decided to investigate this one later. I splashed water on my face and found Ma-ma and Aunt Cat fanning, rocking, and talking on the front porch. I couldn't tell if they had been there the whole time or had napped and returned.

"I'm all fresh again and ready to work," I announced.

"Chér, go help get da yard ready for dinner. Stacy's been a-watching over da cookin' for about an hour; dey should have everything ready by five," Aunt Cat said.

Like clockwork, the dinner was staged minutes before five. The front yard was magical. Large lamps hung from the big oak trees, and small hurricane lamps were placed on each table.

"Oh, it's so good to be with family, yeah." Aunt Cat was sipping Jack Daniel's for "medicinal reasons."

"Oh yeah, chér, it make life good." Ma-ma chimed in. She didn't sip. She was drinking unspiked coffee and rocking. I joined them on the porch, full and satisfied.

As the cicadas began their symphony, Vereen and her daughter recruited a few young cousins to begin offering apple pie, carrot cake, or bread pudding with bourbon sauce. The glow of lights seemed animated as the shine from headlights bounced from an approaching car. It created the familiar crackling sound over the shells that covered the driveway.

"Who is dat?" Aunt Cat sat up a little.

Michael had arrived at about 6:45. He parked, walked toward the now tipsy group, and waved to me as I stood up from the porch swing.

"That's a new friend. I met him last night at Le Bon Temps," I announced.

"Ohhhh, really?" Ma-ma didn't bother to hide her pleasure at the sight of a good-looking man. She straightened her shirt and pants.

Aunt Cat stared at Michael, but her face showed no emotion. I tried to read her face but couldn't. Aunt Cat always showed some level of emotion. A blank face was unusual.

"Hi, everyone," Michael greeted our group.

"Hey, it was good meeting you last night." Stacy walked up to Michael and invaded his personal space. He was friendly but a bit cool toward her, so Stacy returned to her seat next to Robert, humbled and embarrassed. Stacy was not accustomed to being ignored by a man. I felt an inner smile and grabbed Michael's arm as I introduced him to everyone.

"This is Michael Rousseau. He's visiting his aunt and uncle in New Iberia, and we met him at Le Bon Temps. Michael, this is everyone. You will have to go around the tables and introduce yourself. I'll get you a drink, or do you want coffee and dessert?" I asked.

"I will skip dessert, but I would like a Jack Daniel's, rocks," Michael answered.

He followed my instructions and introduced himself to Aunt Cat and Ma-ma first and then circled the tables shaking hands. I handed him a drink, as he was now seated at a table with the men. He added his voice to their man talk of who could drive the longest distance in the shortest amount of time.

"When I hit Virginia, I had beat my time from the last trip," I heard cousin Trey brag.

They reminded me of my father. It was his verbal arm-wrestling to best other men and himself in distance driving or pretty much any topic.

"We had to complete the entire project in three months, *totally* unrealistic.*" Michael's voice had blended perfectly into the space where my father's would have been. He wasn't nervous and had transitioned with the rest into the who-had-the-hardest-job bout.

"Man, that's nothing; we rolled out a whole new system in weeks," my dear brother, Lyle, piped in.

I was amused by the competitive nature of the guys. As Stacy walked past holding a tray of desserts, I was reminded that women compete, too. I rocked with Ma-ma and Aunt Cat, mostly in silence. The young parents were the first to begin leaving. Next, older cousins bid their farewells for the night. Before she left, Stacy had walked over to Michael and touched his hand to say good-bye. She and Robert left. Meeting Michael had numbed the sting of Lance's rejection. He was so smooth and comfortable with people. He was casual and didn't talk like a dictionary. It didn't hurt that he was also gorgeous.

"Tell me, chér, who's ya people?" Aunt Cat dove into her standard preliminary interrogation.

Aunt Cat was wise and sly, and you could tell that she was talking about one thing but watching Michael closely and thinking of another. She was visibly irritated that she couldn't place Michael's family.

"What about Daisy and Harold Rousseau out of Jeanerette? Are you kin to dem?" Aunt Cat was running out of names.

"No, ma'am. I don't know Daisy and Harold. I don't think I'm related to them. My aunt and uncle are Maudry and Dermott. They live on farmland, way outside of Jeanerette," Michael replied calmly.

Aunt Cat continued to study Michael's face as she told stories of mysterious visits from the dead and the many conversations she had had with those who have passed on.

"Catin could always see and hear spirits and get strong visions, better than me. I have only seen a very few visions. They were good ones, but not anywhere near as many as Catin. Everyone around here knows that my sister can see spirits and the future!" Ma-ma was proud of her sister.

Now, I'm embarrassed. Really. Do they have to bring out the family strangeness so soon?

Michael remained polite and interested. Aunt Cat and Ma-ma loved an audience and they moved into talking about the successful spells they had cast in their lifetimes with candles and powders.

"Remember that powder you made for me once, Catin? It really helped my bad back," Ma-ma said.

"OK, that's it!" I felt I had to stop them.

"Enough. This is Michael's first time meeting you. Let's keep the casting of spells and all powders and potions a secret for now," I scolded.

Michael laughed. "Sarah, it's OK. Remember that my family is from Louisiana, too."

I think I was the only one to notice that Aunt Cat shot Michael a look of disapproval when she heard him refer to his family, but she continued to laugh. These looks from Aunt Cat were disturbing. I wanted to know what this was all about. She and Ma-ma said good night.

"What a great family you have. This is so cool. I wish I had more surviving relatives who would do something like this reunion. If we all got together, we'd have fistfights before dessert." Michael grinned.

"Don't be too impressed. We have had our share, but it's usually when somebody dies. In fact, I can't think of many funerals in our family that have gone on without a fight," I said.

We shared funny family stories and then ended the night with coffee and Grand Marnier.

"I better get back to my aunt and uncle's house."

Michael rose from the chair.

"I have to get up early and run some errands, so I better get going. I hope that I'll be moving to LA soon, so can I call if I get the job?"

"Sure. That would be nice," I said.

We said good night, and I watched as he started up his rental car and turned on its headlights. He drove off. I turned around and caught a glimpse of Ma-ma through the screen door. She was looking my way as she came from the hall bathroom. I could see satisfaction in her face.

A UC Berkeley doctorate, a successful practice, but my mom beams when a man comes to see me. He does seem more compatible with me, but that look from Aunt Cat means trouble. I could tell. Sometimes I wonder what exactly they all expect from me. They seem to expect me to have a perfect life. Jesus! I have so much going for myself. Am I to magically produce the perfect man, too? Am I supposed to never make mistakes? I won't ask Ma-ma her opinion, but I want to hear from Aunt Cat. I don't think I'll like what she has to say, but I know that I have to hear it. Damn.

CHAPTER FIVE

The reunion celebration ended as quickly as it had begun. Surprisingly, the dreaded event was a good one for me. I had met Michael. I thought at the time I was incredibly lucky. I learned otherwise later on.

Sunday was a chaotic choreography of long good-byes and promises to stay in touch. Ma-ma and Lyle and his family left before I did. Once back in California, Lyle would drop her off at her place in El Cerrito. Lizette and her husband and daughters followed. They kissed everyone and argued their way to the rental car before backing out and taking the rural road to the highway.

When I had finished packing my rental car, I settled into a chair on the porch for my private good-bye with Aunt Cat.

"Mon chér, I'm so happy to see you looking well and successful. It make me feel good inside, yeah. You know dat your mother is so proud of you, too. She brags about you all da time." Aunt Cat tried to smooth the rough relationship between me and Ma-ma.

"I know. I know. But she just seems ashamed of me most of the time," I said.

"No, chér. And don't ever worry about ya couzan. Stacy is really jealous of you. It's eatin' her up inside. She may be my daughter, but I know dat her weakness is jealousy and spite, yeah." Aunt Cat laughed a big laugh before her tone changed. "You know dat I mean well by you?" she asked.

I nodded in agreement.

"Mon, I'm sorry I have to told you dis, but I had a vision about ya new young man."

Aunt Cat's visions were legend.

"Sometimes…" Aunt Cat began. "…a man is not all bad, but has a bad situation. Das what it is with dis man. He has some bad spirit and a bad situation. I can make you a powder for it, but you have to stay away from him. If you continue to see him, you will be caught up in it, and I can't help you, chér."

"What do you mean *bad spirit?*" I tried not to sound irritated and impatient, but I was.

"I told ya, Sarah, dis don't always come in clear. My vision right now shows that he is a troubled man with a troubled life, and I see you in tears and misery if you stick with dis man. I saw a glow over him as if he was two people, chér. I was looking at you two out of the window, but I saw him in doubles. I think he is hidin' somethin', yeah, and I saw you in tears, big tears." Aunt Cat's eyes glazed over as if she were looking into another world.

"I don't understand, but I thank you, Auntie. I guess I will have to take this in." I fought to hide my disappointment in Aunt Cat's prophecy. Her ability to see into the future could not be argued with, but I wanted her to be wrong this time. Maybe, just maybe, Aunt Cat was not seeing the complete picture.

"Merci beaucoup, Auntie. I will keep my eyes open. I really will. Be well, chér." I kissed Aunt Cat on the cheek and jumped into the car, waved good-bye, and drove off.

What could this be about? Doubles? What does it mean?

Why would I see things so differently? As I neared Lafayette, I quickly took the airport exit. Within an hour, I had returned my rental car and settled into my seat on the plane. I asked for a pillow and a Jack Daniel's and water. I wanted to sleep, but a warning from Aunt Cat, even one I wasn't ready to believe, made it impossible to relax. My visions were finally beginning to reveal more but seemed to be in direct contrast to Aunt Cat's. *Will I ever have the clarity and accuracy of Aunt Cat with my gift of visions? And if so, how will I use the gift? Should I incorporate it into my practice? Would that even be ethical?* I wondered where this was leading.

The cool Oakland air felt crisp, friendly, and easy to breathe compared to the humid Louisiana air. I was tired from the long flight and ready to resume sleep in my own bed. While I waited in line for the shuttle, my stomach turned as I replayed Aunt Cat's warning. The shuttle pulled into the front of my condo building at Lake Merritt. It was nestled between a series of older homes and condo conversions, with quite a bit of new construction by the picturesque lake. My two-bedroom condominium had a home office. I had remodeled the space a few years ago in order to create a large, open kitchen and living room area. My kitchen was equipped with a restaurant-quality stove and utensils. I stocked it with wines from my many international travels. The comfort of my condo embraced my broken spirit as I unlocked the door.

I pointed to a favorite cabernet. *I'll unpack and get to you soon.*

My living room doubled as a prayer and meditation space, and I used an Eastern-style screen to separate the meditation area. I decided to drop my bags and sink into my camel-colored suede sofa. It was flanked with antique pieces. I had a sage-green wing-back chair and two wooden Sheraton chairs. My espresso-colored coffee table was a piece I had found in the Middle East and supposedly had been a table for some sort of ancient ritual. African drums doubled as end tables and lamps. I had created a gallery wall with an eclectic mix of African, Asian, and European-inspired art. My bookshelves were heavily stocked with mystery books, psychology textbooks, and escapist romance novels. A wooden music stand held a variety of sheet music and was placed near a window whose landscape view could pass for a work of art. As I nuzzled my glass, a vision hit like an ice cream headache. I saw myself and Michael in my bathroom. He was shaving while I was putting on makeup. I wanted to see more, but it fizzled before I could grasp hold of the thread.

My vision only seemed to reveal that we would become involved, not how or when. The mystery tugged at my peace of mind throughout my warm bath. I wrestled with my soft sheets with each disturbing thought. Planning to go against Aunt Cat's advice never made for a peaceful night's sleep.

The next morning, I opened my draperies to a breathtaking morning of cool sunlight and a barely gray sky. I was glad that I had decided to take a few days off, so I could have some time to myself after the trip to Louisiana. Soon after my shower and breakfast, I decided to finish unpacking and to release the annoying flashing light on my phone signaling messages.

Beep. "Sarah, it's Lance."

Click. I deleted him at hello.

Beep. "Sarah, you must be—"

Click. I deleted again.

Beep. "Sarah, it's Nikeba. Call me when you get settled. Miss ya."

Before talking to anyone, I went to my meditation spot to begin looking within for answers. I called to my higher source and all of my angels and guiding spirits to show me what was really going on and what I was to learn. Usually, my meditations gave me the sensation of words, not pictures like my visions, so I listened hard and quietly. I heard the words deep within. *No man is your enemy. You will always learn from every experience. You will learn truth from lies. You will grow your spiritual gifts. Remember that all will work well and fine. The blessing is worth the journey.* I felt a sense of peace. But I also felt concern. Growth usually came with some kind of pain, and the last thing I wanted was pain. I was torn. I did not want to stay away from Michael. Aunt Cat's vision and the promise of a growth experience was enough to give me doubts, but I seemed compelled to see it through. I wanted to talk it out. My first move was to return Nikeba's call. Lance was dead to me.

"I thought you would be back by now. How was the trip?"

"Nikeba, I met a guy."

"You always meet guys. You are a hot-man magnet."

"But here's the problem. You know about my Aunt Cat and her talents?"

"Yeah, not always buying it, but know it," Nikeba answered.

"Well, I met him when a bunch of us went out to a club. He came over and met the family the next day, and Aunt Cat had a disturbing vision about him. I'm attracted to him. He's cuter than Lance and not

58

a dork. He's much more my type. It's just confusing. He seems OK, but you know my aunt has a helluva track record," I said.

"From what you've told me, she does. You know that I don't really believe in that stuff. This is a hard one because I'm generally suspicious of anyone until I learn something good about them. Maybe the thing here is to get to know more about him," Nikeba said.

"Funny you say that. I had just decided to pass and not spend or waste any time with him to avoid any problems."

"Without knowing more, I don't have any great pearls of wisdom to drop on you," Nikeba said.

"I know. And I keep going back and forth on it myself," I answered, deep in thought.

After a quick catch-up on Bay Area events and friends, we hung up, leaving the issue of Michael unresolved. I cleaned my place up a bit and went for a jog around Lake Merritt.

Two days later, it was Tuesday late morning. I was at home between errands, and the subject of my angst called.

"How you be, chér?"

"I be fine. Mon, how you be?" I toyed with Louisiana Creole patois, teasingly, giddy from the call. "How's Phoenix?"

"Oh, it's feeling temporary," Michael answered. "I'm calling for two reasons. To tell you that I'm glad I met you and to make it clear that I want to get to know you when I move to LA. I learned yesterday that I will be working at ARCO."

"Congratulations! I'm happy for you."

"I can't wait to get to know you better, Sarah."

"With you moving a bit closer, that might work out," I said.

"Great. I have a meeting in LA coming up this Friday, and I am staying through the weekend. I would like to come up to the Bay Area to see you."

I had started to feel euphoric infatuation, but the feeling was tainted with suspicion because of Aunt Cat's warning, my meditation, and my visions.

"Can I take you out to dinner and we hang out a little while I'm in California?" Michael's deep voice was sexy. My excitement was building. I was about to cautiously probe for Michael's intended sleeping arrangements, when he added, "I could use more rewards points on my hotel membership, so I can stay at my favorite hotel near the Oakland airport."

"That can work. Call me once you've checked into the hotel, and I'll pick you up."

"I'll do that. Bye, lady."

"Bye."

After the phone call, I had new energy and an appetite. I went into the refrigerator and pulled out ingredients to make a Caesar salad.

I think this guy really likes me.

The next day was Wednesday and time for me to go back to work. When I arrived at my office, I discovered my morning appointment had canceled. Ordinarily, I hate last-minute patient cancellations, but things were rolling off my back. In fact, I had taken the rest of my week in the office in stride. Jean never asked about Lance. She had learned that when I stopped mentioning a guy by name, she should not mention him either. I did tell her about Michael.

"You are amazing. You meet men so easily," Jean marveled.

"Yeah, I have that part down. It's the relationship piece that escapes me." I laughed. "But Michael and I have talked on the phone almost every night for hours at a time. He has to be in LA Friday and will come up here Saturday morning to visit me. I'm a little nervous."

"I am hoping for the best, Dr. Sarah."

"Thanks."

Saturday morning, I took an early jog around Lake Merritt and returned to my condo for a shower and shampoo.

The phone chimed.

"Hello?"

"I'm in Oakland. Ready for dinner?" It was Michael.

"It's a little early for dinner, but I will be ready soon. I was out jogging, so believe me, you'd want me to shower first."

"Yeah, you're cute, lady, but funk don't work on anyone. What time do you want me ready?" he asked.

"How's six?"

"Good. See you at six."

Before getting dressed, I took the time to meditate. Although I tried to force one, no visions appeared. After about ten minutes, I gave up. I chose a casually elegant and sexy outfit. I pulled out black evening pants with a strapless red silk camisole top and my favorite black Armani jacket. My shoes were five-inch pumps with thick straps that wrapped my ankles and seemed to say "do me." I wore my dreadlocks down, cascading around my shoulders. I finished with smoky-gray eye shadow and blazing-red lipstick.

OK, this is it. We're getting back on the horse post-Lance. Let's see how this one rides. Oh, no. No sexual innuendo. No sex. No sex. Just dinner.

I was bobbing my head up and down while reciting my platonic oath. I breezed through my parking garage and clicked the key-activated lock of my black Mercedes E-350 and began the drive to the hotel and toward the new adventure called Michael. He was waiting at the valet stand as I drove up.

"You look hot, damn hot!" he added. "Do you want to have dinner here at Oscar's Grill?"

"Sure. Sounds great."

I liked the idea but hoped it wouldn't lead to a premature invitation to his room. I handed my keys to the valet.

We walked into the African-safari-themed restaurant and briefly stopped to chat about the ten-foot mural of countries in Africa. Once we were seated, our conversation floated harmoniously from one subject to the other.

"Did I tell you how good you look?" he asked.

"About five times, but thank you. I love the compliments. You look like traveling hasn't done you any harm," I flirted back, and then we ordered dinner. Our conversation drifted easily into confessions of personal faults and shortcomings.

"I have to admit, I'm anal," Michael owned up.

"You sure you want to admit that to a therapist?" I joked. "To be honest, I'm at the other end of that. I have moments of being hopelessly unorganized." I didn't mind harmless admissions, but I carefully avoided talk about failed relationships.

We laughed and talked for hours, choosing not to break the comfort of each other's company. When I looked back on this night, I realized that I never asked Michael about his relationship history. That was a huge mistake. I had retreated into my pattern of refusing to ask obvious or tough questions. It was my way to not make waves, play it safe. Ironically, I was actually playing dangerously.

"I really don't want to do anything but sit here and enjoy getting to know you." Michael's smile penetrated my skin, and for the first time, I felt a chill of quick fear. He seemed creepy, phony, and forced. I chose to ignore it, attributing it to my vision-influenced imagination. But a glimpse into another side of Michael was revealed when the waiter accidentally spilled water on his hand while refilling his glass.

"Is this how you treat the customer?" he reprimanded.

The waiter was clearly taken aback and gave Michael a hateful look.

"It was not intentional, Michael. I don't like to be too harsh with waiters. They are handling our food and drinks, after all." My voice was soft but firm.

Michael recovered his temper and flashed a quick smile. "You're right. Sorry about that. Guess I'm getting a bit stressed with the move and job change happening so fast, you know."

"I do know. Those are two stressors. You might need more rest." I was now using my soothing, therapist voice.

"And good company helps to calm me, too." He stroked my arm softly.

I changed the subject. "Tell me why you like working in corporate America."

"I know people complain that it's boring, but I really like the structure," he answered.

After another hour or more of conversation, we ended our meal with coffee and Grand Marnier, which had quickly become our tradition.

"Oh, my goodness, I didn't know it was eleven o'clock already." I glanced at my watch.

"Me neither." Michael looked at his watch. "I better let you get home."

What a gentleman. Or is he this polite because he's not really attracted to me? OK, stop it, Sarah.

I stood up. "I guess it is time to go."

Michael stood up, too. He held my hand as he walked me through the lobby of the hotel and stopped suddenly. He leaned in and kissed me so intensely the back of my knees caught a tiny shiver. He pushed his tongue gently past my teeth, and I inhaled him. When the long kiss ended, I stumbled as I started to walk toward the valet stand. I felt another intense chill of fear, but when I turned around and saw Michael's broad smile, I was warmed. I again was silencing my gut instincts. I tipped the valet and waved good-bye to Michael, who continued watching as I drove off. While traveling Hegenberger Road en route home, I felt new confidence and thought, *Lance who?* I was definitely over him now. I gave a symbolic wave to Aunt Cat.

Auntie, your record is falling by the wayside on this one.

I turned up the radio and harmonized with the Eagles' song "I Can't Tell You Why" all the way home.

This feels like a relationship in the making. I just know it. But why do I keep getting goose bumps of fear? This contradiction is beginning to mirror a frequent therapist's dilemma. Our knowledge can often sit in opposition to instincts, further complicated by personal leanings and in my case, visions. And when it involves my personal life, it's nearly impossible to figure out. Damn.

CHAPTER SIX

"**U**h, hmm, hello." My voice was foggy and bass as I was startled from a deep sleep by the phone.

"Good morning, sweet lady!" Michael was gleeful. "Sounds like I woke you, sorry. I'm an early riser."

Great. A morning person. They irritate me.

"No problem," I lied. "Let me just try to open my eyes, and then I can get my mouth to work."

Michael laughed. "I love your wit. I called to see if you have time for an early Sunday lunch today. I have a late-afternoon flight, so maybe we can meet around noon?"

"Sure. How's sushi at Night Jam's near Jack London Square? Then I can take you to the airport for your flight."

"I love sushi, and thanks for offering to take me to the airport." Michael promised to be packed and ready promptly at noon.

Just before noon, I called Michael's cell phone.

"Your car is nearing the hotel, sir," I faked a bad British butler accent.

"Excellent, Giles. Come up to get the bags," Michael played along. "Thanks, babe, I'll be right down."

In the restaurant, Michael and I sat holding hands while talking. I saw a few people at nearby tables look at us and smile. I was a pro with sushi and chopsticks, but Michael gave up and switched to a fork.

When our blissful lunch ended, we zoomed to the Oakland airport, and I pulled up to the terminal curbside. Michael leaned over to kiss me good-bye, and my world felt right.

This matched my vision of driving a man to the airport. This also shelved my fears. I was going to go with my visions over Aunt Cat's warning. This scared the hell out of me, but I was going with it.

Michael completed his move to LA during the next month, and we quickly began dating. Our routine was Michael taking the one-hour flight to the Bay Area, sometimes for one night only. Some weekends, we went to the theater or found other entertainment in and around Oakland and San Francisco. After several weekends, I gathered the guts and invited Michael to hear me sing at Marlin's on the Bay.

"You mean I get to see the famous Sarah Doucette Jean-Louis in action?" Michael teased.

"Yep. And if Chico likes you, you can sit close to the stage," I teased back.

I slowly integrated Michael into parts of my life by introducing him to acquaintances. But I didn't introduce him to Jean just yet. Jean was a loyal employee and casual friend but not as close as my girls and Chico. I waited for him to meet my girls, also. I had to work up to that because if they didn't like him, it would be a strain on all of us. Just when I was close to calling a victory over Aunt Cat's visions of Michael as dangerous, Chico added his words of warning.

"I don't like him. There is somethin' about him that's fake and creepy, girlfriend." Chico didn't hold back.

I pulled the microphone away from Chico so he wouldn't be overheard.

"What do you mean fake and creepy?"

"Can't you see it? This guy is a fake. Physician, heal thyself. Your eyes are closed, Sarah."

"Oh, you never like anyone."

"Not anyone who could be trouble for you."

"He is nice to me. He treats me like a queen. He hasn't been trouble."

"Yet. Humph. He's got a bad vibe, Mz. Girl. Bad. Throw that one back." Chico waved a well-manicured hand covered in diamond rings and made a throw-back-into-the-sea motion.

That's strike two. Aunt Cat and now Chico. They feel something, but what were they talking about?

Chico scrunched his nose and frowned. "I don't like the way he tried to act so familiar when you introduced us. I don't want you to waste your time on somebody like that."

"I think he really is a good guy, Chico. You just don't know him." I fought the defensive sound I heard in my own voice.

"I may not know him, but I can tell that he is a phony. I'm here for you, my sistah, no matter what." Chico turned his attention and jeweled fingers to the piano keys.

I waved and smiled a forced smile in Michael's direction.

Before long, a couple of months had passed, and Michael and I were growing closer in some ways but standing still in others. He had now been living in Los Angeles for a while but hadn't invited me to his place for a visit. He said he preferred being at my place and in the Bay Area. I was glad to be in a relationship, but the warnings of Aunt Cat and Chico remained the backdrop of it all.

One Thursday evening before another weekend with Michael, my mind raced with confusion. I held each of my yoga positions but had to stop when a flash of blue pierced through my head. My stomach turned sour, and the room spun. I saw a huge diamond with spots inside and dirt crusted all over it. I jumped up to try to see more details and hold on to the vision, but it disappeared.

Was this relationship leading up to an engagement? And if so, did the dirty ring mean a dirty engagement? That was hard to believe because over the past few months, Michael and I had not become sexually involved. I didn't push it because after the one-night stand with Lance, I decided to try the three-month rule. No sex for three months, no matter what. *Who the hell came up with these rules?* They usually appeared on the cover of *Cosmopolitan* magazine. I chuckled to myself at the thought of a therapist reading and following the pop psych of *Cosmo*. But I couldn't help but wonder about impotence or some physical dysfunction. I wasn't ready to ask. I hadn't been spending much face time with my girlfriends since I met Michael. I spent my weekends with him or singing. Funny how I always did that when I had a man in my life. They understood and forgave me; after all, they had husbands. Michael was not visiting the following weekend, so I called Nikeba to plan a get-together.

"Nikeba. How's it going?"

"Hi, stranger. The question is, how are you and Mr. New Guy? Every time I talk to you, I can hear you smiling through the phone."

"I tell you the truth. This feels great. I feel comfortable and relaxed. There are just a couple of little things."

"Uh-oh. What little things? He doesn't have a little thing?" Nikeba laughed.

"Actually, I don't know what he has."

"What do you mean you don't know what he has?"

"I mean, I don't know. Never seen it."

"How long have you been seeing him?" she asked.

"Just over three months."

"No sex? No kind of sex?"

"Nope," I said.

"And you don't wonder why?"

"Oh, I definitely wonder…"

"Oh, this calls for a meeting. Chalice, tomorrow at noon?"

"Yep. Noon or sooner."

"I'll call Sandy. Sarah, it will be good to see you. Ciao." She hung up.

The clang of dishes and faint crowd noise in our favorite restaurant was a comfort. I was more bothered than I had let on. Sandy was immediately forgiving about a man she didn't know.

"I think it's kind of sweet. Waiting is special," she said.

We had a full agenda and martinis to get through it. Nikeba and Sandy were the kind of friends every woman should have, two women with their own successful relationships and successful professional

68

credentials. They were both secure enough to share in the happiness of a friend. Ours was a friendship without the competitive undertones that can sometimes characterize female relationships. We had a real sisterhood that spanned more than a decade. We all had mouths like sailors but hearts as big as California. Nikeba Newman and her husband, Steve, had been together for more than twenty years. They met their senior year at Berkeley High School and lived together through college and law school. They got married after graduation. They chose to remain childless because they loved living a strong two-career lifestyle. Both were attorneys with high-dollar practices: her practice in labor law and his in environmental justice. Nikeba was a dark-brown African-American woman, tall and slender like a Senegalese princess. She wore her hair in a short Afro. It complemented her perfectly chiseled face, which was narrow with high cheekbones and deep brown eyes. Nikeba usually wore contact lenses but kept black horn-rimmed reading glasses on hand when she wanted to look lawyerly. She was a Berkeley native. Steve was a salt-and-pepper gray-haired Jewish man with electric hazel eyes. The two made a gorgeous couple, and although of different races, people often commented that they looked alike. They lived in a 1920s craftsman home in Albany, a small city near Berkeley. They updated the house and added a pool in the small yard. It had become a popular entertainment spot for our circle of friends.

Sandra, who preferred to be called Sandy, was taller and thinner than Nikeba and me. She wore her curly red hair in its natural state with an obviously expensive cut designed to look uncut. It was a look reminiscent of 1960s-era hippies. She reminded you of singer/songwriter Carole King. Sandy had grown up in Marin County with affluence and privilege. Her husband of six years, Raphael Acosta, was Chicano and originally from East LA. His family moved up economically and geographically to the Bay Area when he was in elementary school. The two actually met at a nightclub, dated two years, and then got married. Raphael was fashion-model attractive with jet-black hair and eyes to match. He was buff and tanned. Sandy had been a corporate executive working in government affairs, but she became a stay-at-home mom after the birth of their daughter, Marisol, now four years old. Raphael was a contractor whose firm specialized in the restoration of Victorian homes. They lived in one of his best works, a beautiful Victorian kept in its period externally and internally but with contemporary amenities. They lived not far from me in the Bella Vista area of Oakland.

Nikeba blurted, "OK, screw it, I'll ask. Do you think he's gay?"

"Oh, Nikeba," Sandy chastised, "just because a guy doesn't act like a dog, it doesn't mean he isn't attracted to women."

Nikeba locked her eyes and added sarcasm. "Yeah, right. How long was it before Raphael tried when you were first dating?"

"Well…" Sandy hesitated. "N-n-not all men are the same."

We all laughed, remembering how much Sandy had been shocked and fascinated with Raphael's over-the-top sexual enthusiasm.

"Well, that's just how he is. You guys remember how I thought that sex was all Raphael wanted. And, in reality, it may have been. I just managed to hold his interest until he could get to know me and appreciate me for more than just sex," Sandy explained while trying to control her laughter.

"Yeah, I remember you having to take naps so you could hang in there. You were determined to keep the relationship going. You had your legs in the air more than an airline pilot," Nikeba chuckled.

Sandy's embarrassment made us laugh more.

"And I can't talk," Nikeba confessed. "A week after we started dating, Steve told me that he didn't want a platonic relationship. I thought to myself, *This white boy is crazy.*" She laughed at the memory of the early years with her outspoken husband.

Sandy brought the subject back around to me and Michael.

"But this guy sounds like he is really interested in building a relationship. And he seems to be sensitive to the fact that you may have concerns about his intentions." She looked at me for a response.

"Yeah…that could be true. But still. It seems a little out of the ordinary, huh? Plus, Aunt Cat and Chico say he's bad news. They both got a bad vibe from him." I spit it out.

"What? Sarah, I love the stories of your aunt, but are you really going to let frog eyes and lips of newt determine who you date?" Nikeba was harsh about my Louisiana cultural, spiritual stuff.

I rolled my eyes at her and could see that we now had an audience in the busy restaurant.

"We don't use frog eyes anymore. We use lawyers," I shot back in fun.

"OK. Listen, I don't know that I like the guy, but your aunt, the voodoo queen, and Chico, the angry gay man, are not exactly great sources," she reasoned.

"I can't believe that I am agreeing with Nikeba, but it may be too soon to make a judgment call on this. It sounds like he spends a lot of time with you, and you just look so happy. You are glowing."

"Thanks, Sandy. But there are a few questions. Shouldn't a man invite you to his place after a few months?"

"You have never been to his place? I mean, I'm all for giving him the benefit of the doubt, but you haven't been to LA for a weekend?"

"No, ladies, not one trip to LA yet," I declared.

Nikeba was tipsy but trying to focus. "Hmm. Now, that's a different story, and I wonder what that story is."

"Ooooh, Sarah. I'm not sure I am good with that one, either. I just assumed when we hadn't seen so much of you lately that you were trading visits. If he hasn't invited you by now, I think you should ask him why not. You know how you always avoid asking questions when you get involved with a man. You become this unfamiliar shy person. You need to ask about that," Sandy insisted.

"Sandy may be right for once because she agrees with me. Put your cards on the table. Ask," Nikeba said.

"As bold and strong as I can be, I always have trouble asking for what I want from a man or asking anything that could be confrontational or challenging. I don't know why I lose my nerve. You know?" I was talking and reflecting on one of my greatest issues.

"No, we don't know. You sure argue us into the bowels of hell, and you ask us any damn thing, too," Nikeba slurred.

"Nikeba, you are a mess." Sandy had a tipsy giggle.

"I gotta work on this." I was barely listening to them.

"Yeah, you do that. But, Sarah, in the meantime talk to the boyfriend. Not just about easy things, talk about the difficult things." Nikeba ended her sentence with a loud hiccup.

We all sprayed our drinks with laughter.

Nikeba pressed on through slurred speech. She raised her glass in an imaginary toast. "Here's to Michael. After all this time, he damn well better be worth the wait!"

Sandy and I joined the toast.

We had water and coffees to sober us up and left for our homes. I already had a nervous stomach with the thought of confronting Michael. But I had to do it.

CHAPTER SEVEN

Weekends with Michael were now a joyous routine, spending time together at ball games, theaters, the movies, and restaurants—everywhere but in bed.

One evening, after dinner, I took a deep breath and got ready to dig into my tough questions. Before I got the words out, Michael spoke.

"Sarah, I have to ask you something. Are you ready to take our relationship to the next level?"

I didn't want to risk misinterpretation. My body tensed because I didn't want to be let down if he didn't mean what I thought was the *next* level. "What do you mean, exactly?"

"I mean that I like being friends, but I'm ready for more," he explained.

"I want more, too." My smile trembled from its stretch. I later realized that this would have been a great time to stop the physical heat and turn up the questions to Michael. And I realized that I was emotionally immature and not ready for a healthy relationship with a man.

That night for the first time, Michael checked out of his hotel early and spent the night at my place. His walk had a new bounce of confidence; it was almost cocky.

Once at my place, the seduction began. "This is my living room." I led Michael around as if I were a tour guide. "And here we have the kitchen where I make culinary magic."

"I bet you do."

"This is my meditation and yoga area." I continued to walk slowly and seductively.

"I love a spiritual woman." He toyed with me.

If walking can be sensual, we nailed it. We moved together smoothly. It was an omen. We would move together well elsewhere.

"Down this way, you see the hall bathroom and turn left and you see—"

"I see the room where I make magic."

Michael dropped his bags at the door of my bedroom and pulled me close.

He grabbed me around my waist and pulled my lips into his mouth, slowly. He took on the moves of an aggressive but gentle lover, softly leading me onto the bed and slowly pulling off my jean skirt. I felt intense heat and the throbbing of his manhood that comes with arousal. Michael skillfully removed my blouse and bra. His lips found my breasts, and his soft suction sent warm chills up my back. His lips were moist and soft. I helped Michael remove his belt. Once his pants were off, I saw his firm muscles and tight physique. He wasn't overly buff but just enough to look good in clothes and out of them. He guided me backward onto the bed and climbed on top of me. We moved in tight unison until I felt his well-endowed member enter me. My body melted into the sheer force of his movements. I gasped and then groaned and moaned in lightheaded pleasure. It was as if every one of my nerve endings was on fire. I knew this would be special and worth remembering. We both put a lifetime of sexual experience into one night of uninhibited and passionate choreography and climaxed together. We slept, legs still joined.

Michael was up early and dressed before I got up.

"Hey, babe. I had a great night."

"So did I." I couldn't stop yawning. "You're up early."

"I thought I'd jog around Lake Merritt with the other fitness nuts."

He kissed me and left. I made sure he would return to a breakfast of what I called Creole eggs Benedict. It was my own recipe of poached eggs on whole wheat English muffins with melted gruyere cheese, lightly covered with diced shrimp in cream gravy and served with chilled champagne. I was ready to set the table, but Michael had not returned. Even a fitness freak would be back in an hour, but he wasn't. I looked at the clock on my microwave, thinking this breakfast was too delicious and pricey to serve late; it would be ruined. While I kept the food warm, I also was on a slow burn. I was going for my cell phone on the coffee table when it rang. Michael was downstairs waiting for me to give him access back into the building. He must have sensed my near-miss mood because once inside, he freshened up and sat quickly.

"Man! It's like a restaurant in here. Sarah, you are a serious cook, girl."

"Yes, I am." The compliment cooled me down.

Michael picked up his champagne glass, and I noticed a crooked smirk on his face, like a medieval conqueror drinking from his victory chalice. It was disappointing and turned me off. A flash of bright red streaked through my brain. I hid the intensity from Michael. My vision showed Michael with a faceless woman. They were arm in arm and walking up stairs into clouds. This vision pissed me off. It faded before I could react. I pretended to listen to Michael rave about my cooking, but my mind was trying to decipher this latest vision.

"Great lover, great cook, a great woman." He was now overdoing it.

Our first intimate weekend together felt like a moment I was reliving rather than living for the first time. I felt the bittersweet incongruity that would come to characterize our relationship. My good feelings were tainted by my visions, Aunt Cat's warnings, and a frequent chill of unexplained fear. I wanted to ask obvious questions, but I was paralyzed by insecurity and the pressure to have a permanent mate. With Michael, I lost my voice every time. But I always found it with my friends.

"Nikeba, do you think that when you are with Mr. Right, you can have doubts?" I called my best friend once I had my space to myself on a Sunday night.

"There are always doubts. I don't care what anyone says. You sometimes feel like, 'What am I doing?' It's natural. A committed relationship can be unnerving. And forget the movie definition of Mr. Right.

Mr. Right can seem all wrong, and Mr. Wrong can seem so right. Right is what is right for your life, what brings a wonderful balance to an already fulfilled life. That's all the philosophy I have to share." Nikeba ended her speech.

"Hmm. I guess that's the word, *unnerving*. I waited a long time to have someone in my life, and sometimes I wonder if he is really it. Thanks, girl. Talk later." I was a bit dazed.

"You know my fee. Bye, Sarah."

"By the way, he was worth it!" I teased.

"That's one thing about good sex: it can make up for any number of failings. Notice I didn't say shortcomings. Bye. Ha ha..." Nikeba used her rare smiling voice.

"Go, bad girl!"

I didn't tell Nikeba about the vision of Michael with a woman. She wouldn't understand. She thought my visions were crazy. The phone rang and interrupted my thoughts.

"Hello?"

Click.

My caller ID showed a number that must've been Lance's.

What a crazy nerd. Well, now I have a man, so I'll ignore him.

Strangely, a couple of times Lance called, but he only wanted to talk to my voice mail and not with me. When I'd answer, he'd hang up. My caller ID clearly showed Helmington Hospital. I was still pissed at him, so I didn't care what he wanted. He seemed to be caught up in some bashful conflict, but I could not care less now.

I shouted at the phone, "Grow up, Lance. We've all done that call-the-number-chicken-out-if-they-answer thing. But caller ID calls you out! Don't you know that? Clueless."

So let's see, my one-night stand now wants to talk to my answering machine. I'm in a relationship that my psychic aunt says is doomed, and my stalker patient is ratcheting up his game. My life...you can't write this shit!

CHAPTER EIGHT

"**I**'m going to introduce you guys to Michael." I blew the foam to cool my cappuccino and waited for my girlfriends' reactions. Their faces were frozen somewhere between excitement and terror. This particular Sunday we nixed the alcohol and decided to meet for coffee.

"Well, it's about damn time." Nikeba faked anger.

"Yeah. Are you ashamed of us?" Sandy teased.

"No. You know how it is. He is only here on weekends, and there's so little time together. Plus, it's scarier to let him meet you two than my family members. You guys know me so well and know so much about my dating history—I'm just a little nervous that you won't like him. If you don't like him, what do we do then? I would hate that, you know?" I whined.

"Stop whining. It'll be fine." Sandy waved her hand as if wiping my doubts from the air.

"Do you want to sit here, honey?" Nikeba snapped at a woman who was listening closely to our conversation.

I laughed while I chastised Nikeba. "Girl, drink decaf. Leave that woman alone."

"Why are you so grouchy today?" Sandy asked.

"Today? Is she ever not like this?" I stuck my tongue out at Nikeba.

"You two didn't see that woman. She's in my mouth. I'm ready to pull up a chair for her. Anyway, when will this historic event take place?" Nikeba forgot all about the nosy lady at the next table.

"Michael can't come up this weekend. What about the weekend after that, in two weeks? Check with your husbands for Saturday night or Sunday brunch."

Nikeba and Sandy had their phones poised and scrolled to the desired weekend.

"Me and Raphael look better for Saturday night rather than a Sunday," Sandy offered.

"Us, too. Why don't we do a little get-together at my house? I'll talk to Steve. We can order dinner. Sarah, bring a couple of your good wines." Nikeba was in full planning mode.

"Raphael and I can bring all the stuff for martinis, and he'll tend bar."

"Ohhhh..." I shook my head as if hit by a forceful migraine.

"What's the matter, girl?" Nikeba put her hand on my arm.

"Another one, huh?" Sandy asked.

Both friends knew the symptoms of my visions whether they believed in them or not.

This time, I decided to lie.

"No, this was just a quick pain." I didn't want to tell them that the vision included them and showed them both crying. There wasn't enough of a picture for me to answer the predictable questions they'd have, so I kept it to myself. But it was almost as if we were at a funeral. We were crying and wailing in deep grief. I could feel the pain of it, and I wondered who would die. My visions were now starting to scare me. But what do you do with a scary vision? Go to the police? Right. I wasn't sure what to do.

Michael and I kept our phone lines busy in the meantime. Our conversations seem to focus on impersonal subjects, such as the news, politics, and some religion. The time for his next visit had sneaked up on us. Before I knew it, it was time to pick up Michael from the airport.

He flew in on Saturday this time. The LA-to-Oakland flight was a short one, so it worked out. He said that he had to work late on Friday. It was nearly noon when we got to my place. I wasn't happy about him shorting the weekend. But in my Sarah style of avoidance, I didn't want to make waves. We rushed to bed to make love and relax before the dinner party at Nikeba and Steve's house.

I had to pass up the desire to have a lazy afterglow in order to begin getting dressed so we wouldn't be late for the dinner party.

Crash!

"Oh, shit!" My mirror slipped and was in a million pieces. I was not hurt, just startled while trying to rush. "Something crazy always happens when I'm in a hurry," I called out to Michael from the bathroom.

"You are waaay too nervous. This is not that big a deal, just dinner with friends." Michael's cavalier attitude pissed me off.

"Actually, this is a big deal. These are my closest friends in the world. It's as big of a damn deal as if we were meeting our families for dinner—but of course, that's highly un-freakin'-likely, since I have never met any of your family or friends, nor have I even seen your apartment in LA!" I had no control over my resentment. It spilled out in a block of anger.

"Where in the hell did *that* come from? Is this still about the party tonight or what?" Michael was now in a full shout also.

I could feel a combination of helplessness and disgust on my face.

"It is about the fact that we are nearly six months into this, and I feel left out of your life. At the same time, I keep pulling you more into mine. I should have mentioned it earlier because my resentment of this has been building, but I kept thinking you would invite me to LA or at least let me meet someone from your life." I was fighting tears and the intuitive warnings in my gut.

"Hey, hey, I didn't realize this meant so much to you." Michael moved to comfort me. "I told you that I'm clueless about relationships, so I don't know what I'm doing. Listen, I'll fix this. Just let me work out a time when you can come to my place in LA. It's really pretty terrible, but if you are willing to brave it, let's do it." Michael's face turned somber. "I just don't have the kind of life that you have. I have very few friends. I'm not close to my family, so I just don't consider anyone important enough for you to meet. My apartment is new. I'm new to LA, and there's not much to see or do at my place right now. I'm not trying to keep you out of my life; I just don't have much of one right now, babe." He looked sad and frustrated.

"Thank you." I was now calmed. This was a big moment for me. I handled a threatening relationship issue, and we didn't break up. My biggest fear was being dumped, so I tended to avoid conflict at all cost. This was a relationship milestone for me. We finished dressing, went to the garage for the car, and started out in the direction of Albany.

Once in the Newmans' driveway, I asked Michael to get the four bottles of wine from the backseat, and we walked the cobblestone walkway to the front door. I rang the doorbell.

Nikeba and Steve answered the door together, and we all exchanged hugs and greetings.

"Nikeba, Steve, this is Michael Rousseau. Michael, the great couple I've told you about. They are my hearts."

"Come on in, guys, and let me hang your jackets on the hall tree here." Nikeba took our jackets while Michael handed Steve the bottles of wine.

Nikeba and Steve's home had the look and feel of a warm, eclectic experiment. There was a mixture of traditional furniture, custom-made contemporary pieces, and even a chair that looked a bit like a lion. They loved it all, from the conventional to the contemporary. Waitstaff from the catering company took drink orders while we all sat down in the living room.

"This place is very unusual. It's cool," Michael started the conversation.

I was proud as he, again, eased in and out of each conversation with grace and intelligence.

I think I love him. I realized suddenly that, in our six-month relationship, the word *love* had never been expressed. But my somber thoughts were diverted when the sound of the doorbell was accompanied by the playful knocking of Sandra and Raphael Acosta.

Nikeba ran to open the door. "It's the people who are always late," she yelled playfully while she opened the door.

"Hey, we can hear you through that door, you know!" Sandy and Raphael laughed.

"That is the point!" Nikeba teased her friends. "And they try to hang CP time on us—" Nikeba laughed.

"OK, my love," Steve broke in, "let's leave the stereotyping to us white folks." Steve's sense of humor was as irreverent and sarcastic as Nikeba's.

"Yeah," Sandy, as the other white person in the group, chimed in.

Raphael had walked over to Michael and introduced himself.

"Hey, since the rest of them are more interested in their stand-up act than manners, I am Raphael Acosta. Man, good to meet you."

"Great to meet you, also. Michael Rousseau."

Sandy walked over and hugged him as she introduced herself.

I took another moment to enjoy my promotion from fifth wheel. I had had few relationships that left my bedroom long enough to participate in social activities, and this one was the most important. It would be a perfect moment if I could stop thinking that Michael was hiding something. But in this moment, I really didn't want to know. I would worry about it tomorrow.

By month seven, Michael and I were an established couple. We had even had dinner a few times with Ma-ma and with my sister and brother. Michael continued to put off the subject of my weekend visit to LA, but after he talked of the barren apartment, I had lost interest in going. Our lives seemed more centered in the Bay Area. On this particular weekend, Michael left the condo for a couple of unexplained hours. He had been going on jogs that felt too long, but this one was a record even for him. When he returned, my face was hot with anger. Michael was oblivious and walked in with Chinese takeout in large bags.

"I'm doing dinner tonight," he announced. "I can't hold a candle to your cooking skills, so I picked up some of our favorites. Don't you love the moo goo and shrimp fried rice?" He emptied bags and took out plates and forks.

I reluctantly reached for a plate and some silverware with my anger building into confrontation level, which I would go with this time.

"But wait a minute! I want to break tradition and open our fortune cookies first," he insisted.

I was not feeling playful but went along with it.

"This one is yours…and this one is mine." Michael doled out the two cookies, making what seemed to be an unnecessary presentation.

"Open it," Michael ordered. He was far too happy and almost wild-eyed. "Open it!" he persisted.

I matter-of-factly began to open the crispy shell and didn't believe what I saw. Out from between the crumbles dropped a two-carat, princess-cut diamond flanked by sapphire baguettes. The diamond's sparkle caught the tears that welled up in my eyes. I could barely speak.

"Oh, my God! Is this…? Are you…? Oh, my God…I…can't…" I sniffled. "…believe this…" I had become incapable of completing a sentence.

"Believe it." Michael grabbed my hands and knelt down.

"I love you, Sarah. You came as an unexpected surprise in the same way that this ring fell from the fortune cookie. You have added so much to my life. You are the beginning of a new life for me, and I hope that you will make me a happy man by becoming my wife."

"Yes!" I cut him off. "I have never loved any man this much before. Even when I thought I was in love in the past, I was wrong. I know that now. I will be so proud and happy to be your wife." Tears lined my face. I finally had the brass carrot, as I had irreverently nicknamed marriage proposals. For the first time in my life, someone had asked the question I thought I'd never get to answer. I was in the secret club. We began our engagement in bed, moving there to seal the commitment. Immediately following our lovemaking, I told Michael that I had to get to the phone. It was time to share and scream like a girl. Michael laughed and went into the kitchen to finish the barely touched Chinese takeout.

I called Nikeba and Sandy first. We laughed and cried. Michael yelled a quick hello, but he was in the background, literally and figuratively, and he turned back to his now-cold dinner.

I drew in a deep breath and began my call to Aunt Cat. I wanted to get the faster calls done before calling Ma-ma because that call would be the longer one, filled with joyous tears and excitement. She would also want to begin planning immediately.

Knowing Aunt Cat's visions and warning of danger about Michael, I was nervous.

"Auntie! Auntie! I have some news for you, chér!"

"Well told me then, ti Sarah?" Aunt Cat played along, but I was sure she had already figured it out.

"I'm getting married! He asked me! He asked me!!" I began to sob once again.

Aunt Cat's voice didn't sound happy, but she faked it. "I'm happy to hear your happiness, chér. You come to visit me real soon now."

"I will, Aunt Cat, and do me a favor, let the others know, especially Stacy."

We both laughed at the thought of Stacy's jealousy and resentment of any happiness in my life. We talked a little more and hung up.

I stood by the phone for a moment and decided to make the most of this next call by beginning with a touch of drama.

"Ma," I hesitated. "I have something to tell you."

I could hear impatience in Ma-ma's voice. "What's it about? What happened? What's wrong?"

"Nothing is wrong. I just have to tell you some news."

"What?" She was not happy with being teased.

I shouted into the phone and was surprised at how freely the tears kept flowing from my eyes. "Michael has asked me to marry him. I'm getting married!" The words felt foreign to my mouth.

"This is wonderful, Sarah!" My mother's voice became over-whelmed with a combination of emotion and pride. This was the *big one* for her. My mother immediately segued into planning. It was amazing how quickly she could pull together the smallest details on a moment's notice. I guess she had been waiting forty years for this and had stored these plans in the back of her mind. I didn't hear her because I had started to zone out. I was overwhelmed with happiness and the feeling of validation. But even this moment couldn't drown out the words of warning from Aunt Cat after she first met Michael. I glanced at the attractive man while he ate and wondered if I really knew all I needed to know about him.

CHAPTER NINE

"It is so weird. I do all the same things I did before, but it's all different now. Traffic? I don't care; I'm engaged. Late patients? I'm not bothered; I'm engaged! You know?"

Jean listened to me prattle on. "I do. I do understand, Dr. Sarah, and I am so glad you have someone special in your life. I can't wait to meet him."

"You will. I think you'll like him," I said.

"I wonder if you should tell Corwin. He might freak out. He'll be here in a few minutes." Jean was cautious.

"Corwin is the last thing on my mind. He'll have to get over it. I am wearing this beautiful ring," I said, determined.

Jean's concerns proved accurate. In his session, Corwin moved the floppy part of his oversized straw hat from the top of his brow and asked about my ring.

"That looks like an engagement ring." He glared.

"It is, Mr. Corwin. I'm getting married," I said softly.

"Well, that's awful. How dare you? How dare you? How dare you do this to me!" He got up and stormed out of my office. But he stopped at Jean's desk before leaving.

"You do have me for next Wednesday at my usual time, right?" he asked.

"Yes, I have you down at your usual time," she said.

"Good." He huffed and pouted and left.

"That went well," I remarked dryly.

"Don't joke, Dr. Sarah. I think that man is dangerous. It is time to let him go," Jean warned.

"I will have a talk with him first. I was going to deal with him months ago, but I've been distracted. I'll handle it. No worries," I said, trying to soothe Jean's fears.

The following weeks were a blur. I neglected to speak to Corwin, putting it off to deal with Michael. Michael invested extra time in courting Chevron in San Ramon, a suburb of the Oakland area. His networking paid off, and he was offered a job there. He had told his Atlantic Richfield boss that we were getting married, and he said they understood his need to move to Northern California.

Before long, Michael had moved into my place and was commuting to San Ramon and his new job. My life was a cocoon of warmth. Ma-ma and I were knee-deep in wedding planning. But my visions and instincts continued to nag me. For some reason, the engagement I had dreamed about all my life had begun to feel less dreamy. Shortly after moving in, Michael started coming home later and later. His jogs around the lake seemed to take longer and longer. It was the worst time for it because it seemed Jean had been right about the freakishness of Corwin. It was about seven o'clock in the evening when I looked out of the window for Michael, and I caught glimpses of Mr. Corwin outside. I had told Michael, but he didn't seem to take it seriously. I decided to confront Corwin one night and threaten him with the police.

"Mr. Corwin, I see you behind that tree! Come out. Come out and talk to me," I shouted.

"You will be sorry that you have him here." Corwin kept pointing his finger at me while holding a construction hat on his head. He ran away while continuing to shout his threats. "You will be sorry. You'll see, Miss Doctor. You will be." He ran away while replacing the construction hat that kept falling off of his head.

"I will not have you as a patient. That is it. I'm through. I am tired of this weirdness. I am sending you to a colleague!" I yelled. "I mean it, Corwin." I was now afraid of the stalker with the gentle voice and disturbed mind.

The next morning, I made good on that threat and sent Corwin, his hats, and his files to a colleague in Berkeley. He was gone. I hoped.

CHAPTER TEN

While I waited for Ma-ma at the caterer's place, I stared into space thinking of my two major problems, Michael's changing behavior and Corwin's threats. The caterer's voice pulled me back into the room. "Ms. Jean-Louis, we have you scheduled to taste five selections: the lemon mousse wedding cake, the champagne and strawberry cake, a variation of the Louisiana chocolate doberge cake, the romantic marble, and the traditional white cake with white chocolate filling. Is that correct? Ms. Jean-Louis?"

I snapped out of my reverie. "Oh, yes. Those are correct. I'm waiting for my mother, and she'll be here any minute."

Ma-ma rushed in on cue and was taking her coat off a little out of breath.

"OK, Sarah. This is the fun part. How many cakes will we be tasting today?"

"It's these five." I showed her a list.

"OK, let's start."

The caterer was smiling and signaled for her staff to begin serving bites of the heavenly pastry creations.

"Oh, my God!" I tried not to sound orgasmic in front of Ma-ma, but the soft, creamy sweetness was overwhelming.

"Ummmmm, ummm..." Ma-ma exaggerated the smacking of her lips and laughed. "This New Orleans doberge is to die for...ummm, umph!"

"Oh, yeah. But so are all of the others. They are all fantastic. I think the champagne-and-strawberry cake is it, though. What do you think?"

"Yeah, yeah, that's it! Yeah, chér, that champagne and strawberry is perfect, and in a funny way, it will go with your colors." Ma-ma was trying to talk and eat at the same time, while she scooped more of the moist cakes onto her plate.

"I'm so ashamed of myself." Ma-ma pointed to her bloated stomach. "This was supposed to be just a tasting, and shoot, I had dinner!"

We laughed like best friends and went to a nearby coffee shop to go over wedding plans for the two-thousandth time. Ma-ma loved talking about and rehashing the wedding plans.

"We still haven't chosen the flower girl dress for Sandy's daughter, Marisol," I reminded Ma-ma.

"Did you talk to your sister about standing as matron of honor?"

"Yeah, Ma-ma, I talked to Lizette, and of course, she said yes. Sandy and Nikeba will be bridesmaids."

"I know the wedding is ours to plan, but is Michael's family going to play a role at all?" Ma-ma asked.

"Well, they are estranged, Ma-ma. I don't like it, but he says he doesn't want any of them in it. He may invite a few of them, though. He's thinking it over."

"So who will be his groomsmen? This is pretty strange." Ma-ma frowned.

"He wants Lyle, Steve, and Raphael."

Ma-ma made a disapproving face but immediately dismissed any concern. I saw clearly where I had inherited the head-in-the-sand trait.

"What about the Tom Thumb wedding?"

"That is just corny, Ma. Nobody does that anymore." I sounded like a child again, whining in protest.

"Oh, but a Tom Thumb wedding is so cute. I just love seeing the little toddlers dressed like miniature versions of the bride and groom."

My mother had gone from zero to sixty in her steel-magnolia style. She smiled and then zoomed into short, angry phrasing. "It will be lovely, and anyway, when did I ever care what other people do?" She held her ground.

"Well, we sure can't call it a Tom Thumb wedding. That is not appropriate, but junior bride and groom or junior wedding party, whatever."

I sensed that I had lost the argument and embraced the fact that this wedding was not actually mine but Ma-ma's.

"Ohhh, how lovely. When people see your nieces and nephew walk down the aisle at the beginning of the ceremony dressed like the grown-up wedding party, they will just melt!" Ma-ma was excited and single-minded.

"All right, Ma-ma, we'll get outfits for them and have them walk down the aisle in front of me. It'll be cute," I acquiesced.

I couldn't help but think of the Carl Jung quote, "Nothing has a stronger influence psychologically on their environment and especially on their children than the unlived life of the parent." It seemed to have been written about Ma-ma's unlived life. Despite it all, I watched her through kind eyes. I knew it was more important to enjoy this time with my mother than to engage in a power play.

"Well, we better go. You sure you won't come to the couples' shower, Ma?"

"You said the words, 'couples' shower.' I am not part of a couple anymore. I'm happy to stay home and get some rest. But I had a fun day with you, chér."

My mother wasn't much of a partygoer, so I knew she wouldn't want to go to the shower that Nikeba and Sandy had planned. We walked to my car.

"I can catch BART from here, Sarah." Ma-ma was walking ahead.

"No way, Ma. It's not that far. No need to take the train. It's getting a bit late. I can take you home and still get to the party in time. Go ahead and get in. I have to make sure you get home fast; you look like you're about to pop from all of that cake!" I laughed.

"Why the hell did I eat like that?" My mom gave a laugh that was bigger than her usual chortle. She got into the car. I dropped her off, went home, and changed, and I was just in time to be guest of honor for the grand engagement party.

Nikeba and Sandy had thought of everything. There was a digital clip of me and Michael on the widescreen TV on a continuous loop. They had hosted this soiree at my favorite Berkeley landmark, the Royal Vista Hotel, at the base of gorgeous hills with its top-shelf atmosphere. Nikeba and Sandy saw me walk in and came straight in my direction for a group hug.

"This is breathtaking. You guys have outdone yourselves." I complimented them.

"We wanted the best for our best friend," Sandy said.

"Have you guys seen Michael yet? He said he had to work a little late but would meet me here," I asked.

"No, we haven't seen him; we'll look. Move around and have fun, we have to talk to the caterer for a minute." Nikeba and Sandy walked off.

Steve came up to me for a dance and wouldn't take no for an answer.

"I haven't danced with you in a long time." Steve smiled.

"True. It's been years. Oh, I see Michael. I was wondering when he'd get here." I looked around while dancing.

"Oh, good, where is he?" Steve asked.

"He's talking to Jean. Guess they introduced themselves...Hey, Travolta, don't bring disco back on my account." I poked fun at Steve.

"You just can't keep up." He laughed.

During the disco spin, I lost sight of Michael and Jean for a minute. He seemed to yell at her. It was bizarre. I couldn't hear anything, but it looked strange. When the music stopped, Steve went for a drink, and I looked for Michael.

"Hi there. My two favorite people have met finally."

Jean looked visibly shaken.

"Yes, we did meet. Um, I'm going to get a glass of wine. See you in a few, Dr. Sarah, Michael." She nervously walked away.

"Hi, babe. How's my lady tonight?" Michael was overly cheery. He kissed me softly.

"Michael, do you want something to drink? I just danced, and I'm thirsty." I hinted for him to get me a drink.

"No, I have to find the men's room. I'll catch up with you." He did not pick up the hint and seemed distant.

Jean's expression bothered me. I found her near the buffet table.

"Jean? You looked upset. What happened? Was it something with Michael?" I asked.

"Oh, no, I was feeling funny, but the wine is settling my stomach. I probably waited too long to eat."

I could tell that Jean wanted to get away from me. She seemed different, but I let it go when one of my old college buddies asked to dance. It was, after all, my party.

The girls later told me that, ironically, my engagement party and Jean's chance meeting of Michael signified the beginning of the end. Jean had explained to Sandy and Nikeba what she would not tell me initially. She explained that when she finally met Michael, he looked familiar. She thought she recognized Michael from her old Cal State Northridge days. The name seemed different, but he looked like a guy whose insanely jealous girlfriend became pregnant; they had gotten married. At the party when Jean asked Michael if he went to Northridge, he became nasty and even pushed her out of the way. That extreme behavior caused Nikeba to ask Steve to run checks on Michael, and the girls became amateur sleuths. I had complained of Michael's late-night jogging, so they began following him from Lake Merritt. What they discovered about him would change every aspect of my life forever.

CHAPTER ELEVEN

They made up a story about Sandy to get me to meet at Nikeba's. Because of my fledgling engagement, I had begun isolating myself and I was refusing invitations from the girls. Jean was there to "help."

Michael had been staying out late and growing more distant. We had decided that he should take an apartment in San Ramon to reduce his commute and the strain that was building on our relationship.

I had even toyed with the idea of ending the engagement or at least postponing the wedding. I tried to talk it over with Ma-ma, but she flew into a rage over the phone.

"Are you *crazy?*"

"It's not crazy to have serious doubts and concerns about marrying someone."

"Men are hard to deal with, Sarah. You don't need to do anything so drastic. So, he's acting a little crazy. He's probably got cold feet. You have to tolerate men. Sometimes you have to ignore and do things you might not ordinarily do. These are your pushed times; they'll pass."

"What does that mean, my 'pushed times'? You have never told me about that before."

"Pushed times make a monkey chew pepper. It means that in hard times, we do things out of necessity that we might not ordinarily do. These are your pushed times. It will get better," Ma-ma answered.

"That just doesn't sound very comforting."

"Don't call it off, Sarah. You'll be a laughingstock." Ma-ma said a few more insulting things, and I let her hang up.

I was angry but too depressed and confused to attack her for that remark. I wondered if other brides-to-be faced this amount of doubt and disappointment. But my girls answered my feelings of doubt with information that would literally bring me to my knees.

"Sarah, we will be honest," Nikeba began carefully.

"This brunch is about problem solving but not Sandy's problems. We just said that because we knew it would get you over here."

I had noticed that they were solemn. I also noticed that Jean was present, and she never came to our brunches.

"True," Sandy added her one word.

"We have information that will answer any questions you have about Michael. The things he hasn't told you or won't tell you..." Nikeba tried to steady her voice.

"What do you mean about Michael? Where would you guys get information? And why would you have information?"

"Sarah, forget those questions. We have information that is bad. Really bad," Nikeba spoke slowly.

"We waited a while to share this..." Sandy was beginning to tear up.

"What do you mean? I don't expect this gossipy girl shit from you guys! You're not like that. You're not like the horrible bitches we know who have to try to ruin other people's happiness. What do you mean?" My head was spinning, and I began to ramble.

Nikeba was now holding my hands, and Sandy was rubbing my arms.

"Steady yourself. This is big, and we already know that it's all true." Nikeba was now crying.

I pulled my arms and hands away.

"I know I'm down today, but I'm getting married after years of disappointment and bad bridesmaid's dresses—no offense. It's stressful, OK? Don't do this to me. To my dream. Don't do this!" I cried. I knew the visions, the warnings, the suspicions were all coming to a head now. I didn't want to know it. I didn't want this fantasy engagement to end. My gut had won out. Aunt Cat was 100 percent accurate, as always. I knew it was over.

Nikeba took a deep breath and began to deliver her recitation, devoid of emotion. She placed photo after photo on the coffee table—delivering fact, chapter, and verse.

"Jean told us she recognized Michael from Cal State Northridge, but he nearly attacked her at the engagement party when she mentioned it.

Jean explained, "I didn't want to tell you the night of the party, Dr. Sarah, but he really pushed me. I knew he was the same Michael then. If not, why get so mad?"

"So, I had a police check run on him. The fact that he seemed to keep his life so secret from you, coupled with Jean's suspicions...we just thought it would be best to check him out," Nikeba interjected.

"And what? What did your checks find? What are you saying?" I felt panic rush through my body. "Just fucking tell me!" I was shouting.

"He's married, Sarah. He's married. He has kids, and they all live in San Ramon," Nikeba blurted it out through sobs.

"No. That's the wrong guy."

I refused to hear it. But the photos and files made it obvious. I saw Michael with his wife and family in front of the apartment, at a park, and leaving Lake Merritt. I saw him being picked up by his wife. I fell to the floor, my chest heaving as I wept uncontrollably.

"This can't be. This can't be. This is a fucking nightmare." I sobbed until my ears throbbed and I was drenched in tears.

Nikeba, Sandy, and Jean wept just as hard while my body trembled in pain. We spent what seemed forever in silence, except for the sounds of crying. In tragedy, triumph. I was learning to interpret my visions and recognize their manifestations—the vision of us crying, the death of my engagement and my dream of getting married. This was the funeral in that vision.

I turned bloodshot eyes to Nikeba. "Tell me the rest. Tell me what all of this means." I was a zombie and wiped my eyes in vain.

"Her name is Denise. She was in school with us at Cal State Northridge years ago." Jean picked up the story. She drew in a deep breath and continued, "Back in the day, in college, we knew a girl named Denise; in fact, we sorta hung out in the same crowd. She was big-time in love with a guy named Michael. We used to tease her about her Louisiana man since his family was from Louisiana and he had a French last name. Well, Miss Denise took no chances. She really, really wanted him, so she got pregnant and they got married. Denise was one of those really cute girls who seemed a little crazy—not funny crazy but lay-on-a-couch crazy. She was extremely jealous and would stalk Michael if he was with any other girl. She was way off the deep end. About a year ago, I was in LA with some old college friends, and we caught up on who's where and what from the old days. Since I didn't finish school, I would always ask about the people who stayed after I left. I asked whatever happened to crazy Denise and her Louisiana man. We never said his last name so I forgot what it was, but at the party, it hit me that this guy looked like *that* Michael, only twenty years older.

"Their name is Rochon, not Rousseau. He never lived in Phoenix. He has always lived in LA. In fact, he grew up in LA." Jean talked while sniffing and fighting back tears.

"Once we got the correct name, we began more in-depth research. We followed him from his jogging around the lake to San Ramon," Nikeba continued. "We would call you to find out when he was jogging and take it from there."

I looked through the files and saw copies of a marriage license. I was in shock.

"Do you know what is going on? Is this some kind of scam?" I asked weakly.

"We haven't been able to figure that part out," Sandy answered. "We were concerned it may be about your money."

I looked again at the collection of photos. Even in my unhappiness, I had not imagined this kind of pain or level of deception. It was too big and too deep to blame the girls. I closed my eyes and sobbed so hard I began to lose all sense of time and space. The tears and water that poured from my eyes, nose, and mouth caused me to choke, but I didn't try to recover. I just wailed. I fell to the floor and grabbed my stomach and heart and became part of the wood floor. I never thought anyone would ever hurt me this bad. I never thought anyone would hate me this much. And I was going to marry him. Now all of the visions made sense: Aunt Cat's doubles—two last names; the dirty engagement ring—a filthy, lying bastard of a fiancé; our weeping…It was all coming together.

"Give me a drink, please, a strong one." I needed to be numb.

Nikeba didn't bother with glasses, and the four of us took big swigs from a bottle of Jack Daniel's.

Through red, swollen eyes and faces, we drank in silence.

Finally, Nikeba broke the silence.

"There's more. My sources sent me this information just yesterday. When you met Michael, you said he told you he was visiting relatives in Louisiana? Well, he could have been, but we did Louisiana research where he is listed as the father of a toddler there. It appears he did not marry the woman but signed the birth certificate. We had someone call under the pretense of selling insurance, and the woman said Michael did not live there because he was an airline pilot, living in California. That poor woman sounds gullible." Nikeba shook her head.

In light of the situation, Nikeba seemed to instantly regret her last words, but she couldn't take them back.

"Yeah, probably not as worldly and educated as I am...the great and wise me! The great and wonderful therapist—" I was about to begin a bitter speech when Sandy stopped me.

"Stop it!" Sandy was trying to sound strong as she cried, "You just stop it! You are great, and you are wonderful, and I'm not going to let you blame yourself for the actions of an asshole, a criminal!"

"Now it makes sense that Aunt Cat could not trace the name Rousseau and match Michael with a family there. If he had given her his real name, she would have been able to get the whole story. I am a stupid old fool who is so eager to get married I refused to deal with tough questions. I don't know what this was about for him."

I searched my education and training for some kind of explanation, but I was in no condition to diagnose. Then an idea came to me that gave me a shiver of evil excitement.

"You know, I can get married and maybe I will," I declared.

"What?" Sandy, Nikeba, and Jean couldn't believe their ears.

"How in the world is that a good thing?" Nikeba asked forcefully.

"Sarah, you're drunk," Sandy tried to say delicately.

"No, I'm not drunk. Think about it. He has to be a bigamist to go to prison. I'm going to help him get there. This would be the ultimate performance, a paradoxical moment of truth and deception that would now be carried out by both of us. But the difference is I win," I resolved wickedly.

My friends carried looks of shock and disbelief. I didn't tell them, but I felt the same way. I couldn't believe what was coming from my own mouth. But I also couldn't stop it. Not then.

CHAPTER TWELVE

Monday morning at the office, I tried to avoid the sympathy in Jean's eyes.

"Dr. Sarah, your plan still may not be the best thing for you. Please, don't do it. This is not what you would tell one of your patients to do," she pleaded.

"But I'm not a patient; I am the one hurting and dying inside. I can't be my own therapist. I have to follow my feelings. He has to be stopped. I have to see him in prison. I have to make sure he gets there." I squeezed my still bloodshot eyes shut.

"But what if he turns dangerous when he is exposed?" She was pleading.

"I never see him anymore. He is rarely at my place these days, and now I know why. Humph."

"Why are you so hell-bent on doing this?" Jean was confused. "You will have to fake your entire life until the wedding."

"I'm helping somebody! And I'm helping myself! Sometimes you do difficult things in difficult times. Pushed times make a monkey chew pepper—that's what this means and what this time requires."

"Pushed what?" The explanation left Jean more confused.

"Never mind." I went into my office and slammed the door.

That evening, more bad news came. Stacy called to let me know that Aunt Cat had become ill and was growing weak.

"The doctors say her heart is weak, and it's mostly her age," Stacy's voice had the sound of someone who had been crying all day.

"When did all of this start?"

"Chér, my mama never liked the doctors, you know, but she has been having horrible chest pains for about six months. We finally got her to go to see the doctor, and they did some tests. That was last month. She wouldn't let us tell anybody. They found some blockage in her arteries, but the doctors said at her age, almost a century old, they can't really think of operating on her." Stacy began to cry. "I know people say she already lived a long life, but nobody wants their momma to leave."

"That is so true, Stacy."

"I already talked to your momma. She is making her travel plans and asked me to call you."

"I'll be there as soon as I can; don't worry." I hung up the phone and sat motionless.

Does it have to pour when it rains? Why now?

I picked up the phone to make travel arrangements, and I called Jean to let her know I would be leaving for Louisiana immediately.

"Don't worry, Dr. Sarah," Jean's comforting voice calmed me.

"I'll make sure your schedule is all taken care of. I'll reschedule patients and work things out. You just go; we can talk later." Jean hung up.

I was glad that Michael was at his apartment, obviously with his wife and family. I played the role, by calling to let him know about Aunt Cat. He faked concern and an offer to go with me to Louisiana. I begged off and said it was something I had to do alone.

I closed my eyes to think back on my times with Aunt Cat and the first time she explained my gift of visions, back when I was a little girl.

"Ti Sarah. Vien wa ici, chér."

"Yes, Aunt Cat."

"You keep talking about pictures in you head, yeah. Let me told ya what dat mean. Dat mean you have a gift. You can see messages from God, yeah. Most folks just hear dem in their heart, but you see and hear dem. It is a very, very special gift, mon chér, and you never, never use it for evil. It don't work for evil, cuz it's from God, who is good."

"What do you mean use it for good? I don't understand, Auntie."

"I mean, you use the pictures to help people or help yourself learn what you need to know in life. Close your eyes and see what you see." Aunt Cat was a skillful teacher.

I closed my eyes and saw myself playing in my backyard in California on the swing. I was so excited.

"Aunt Cat! Aunt Cat! I went to my backyard in California, and I was swinging, and I went there without the airplane!"

Aunt Cat laughed. "Dat's the gift! And sometimes, pictures real like dat will come into your head and you have to let it play. If you ignore it, day won't come. If you sit and watch and listen, day will flow like a little movie. Oh, mon chér ti bebe, I'm so glad somebody got da gift since none of my children did. You a good child, ti Sarah."

Tears streamed down my face as I relived that moment. I realized that even in my grief, I was blessed with an unbelievable and rare gift that I was now determined to learn to use. This gift had fallen neatly into my educational training. I finally accepted that this part of me and my heritage could enhance my ability as a therapist and my life as a woman.

I walked onto the plane and sat in my seat. Aunt Cat's illness forced me to put Michael's deception on the back burner, and that was a good thing. My battered heart needed to hear and feel the presence of Aunt Cat before she crossed over, and that was all I could think about.

I had finally landed and was driving to see Aunt Cat at the hospital. Ma-ma was already there, and other family members would arrive throughout the week.

I parked the rental car and took the elevator to the third floor waiting area of Franklin Doctor's Hospital. I looked around the waiting room at my family.

"I know that my momma has had a long life, but I still don't want her to go." Stacy wept.

I couldn't help but feel sympathy for the cousin who spent a lifetime besting me and never missing an opportunity to embarrass and berate me over the years. But this was not a time for old wars or new wounds; this was a time to speak with Aunt Cat and celebrate her long life one final time.

We took turns going into Aunt Cat's room. I walked in quietly and couldn't believe the frail woman hooked up to tubes was my vibrant Aunt Cat.

"Como ca va, Auntie?" I whispered.

"Bien, chér, bien," she answered in a weak voice. "I know they are out there with their long faces and sympathy for themselves, but, chér, I have lived a long and very blessed life. The only reason I allowed them to bring me to the hospital is so that I would not die in my house or anyone else's house—I don't like that."

I smiled at her strength and fearlessness.

"But I have to know, are you still going to marry dat man? Don't do it. It don't worth it. And dat's all I'll say."

"Aunt Cat, I have found out everything. He is married already. I can't believe how horrible he is and that I didn't know it until now. My girlfriends figured it out and told me." The words caused me to cry all over again. "I'm sorry."

"Don't be sorry. You are not da fault here. I found dat out, too, a few days ago after talking to some people around here. He's a Rochon, not a Rousseau! He's trouble and married." Aunt Cat was now speaking freely.

"I know, Auntie, I know. But that is not for you to worry about. I will handle it."

Aunt Cat insisted upon continuing. "I found out just before I took sick. I couldn't find a way to call you and keep it just between us, you know? I hope you call that wedding off. It's better to just be free of him. He could hurt you even more, chér. But what I want you to know is dat he is about to face his deeds. He is, so stay away from him so you don't get caught up in da mess. You'll be fine. Just get away, and stay away from him! I saw a vision, and he is about to pay for his deeds, yeah."

Aunt Cat tried to rise up in her bed and then relaxed again, having made her most important point to me.

"OK, Auntie. You don't get yourself excited. I will handle it. Mon Auntie, did you put a spell on Michael?"

Aunt Cat's voice became strong and feisty again.

"Don't ask me my business," she shot back.

We both laughed.

"Now, ti Sarah, go ask da nurse to come here. I have a pain in my side." She sent me out of the room.

I jumped to attention and ran down the hall to the nurse's station.

"Come quick, please. My auntie needs you!"

The other relatives heard me, and the entire group headed to Aunt Cat's room.

When we entered the room, it felt different. Aunt Cat looked as if she were taking a peaceful nap, but her spirit had left her body. I knew then that she had intentionally made me leave the room before taking her last breath. Quiet tears ran down all of our faces. Aunt Cat was gone. Nothing would be the same in Louisiana without her.

We went through the motions at Gramp's house, cleaning the kitchen and preparing for bed.

During the next few days, Ma-ma and I helped Stacy and her sisters and brothers prepare for Aunt Cat's funeral. The service was brief and conducted as a celebration of Aunt Cat's life. Stacy took it particularly hard. She was the youngest of Aunt Cat's children.

No one mentioned much about Michael other than to ask why he couldn't come. I told them he couldn't get away from the job. Family members and friends gave testimonials about the life that had impacted their rural community for nearly a century. Aunt Cat did not approve of organized religion, so rather than a Catholic Mass, a small ceremony was held at the funeral home.

To the surprise of the family, I declined to offer a testimonial during the service. They did not know that I was grieving more than one death and speaking publicly would have been impossible.

At the interment, I watched sadly while the casket with Aunt Cat's body was raised into a family mausoleum. The whole thing was surreal.

Gramp's house was the setting for the postfuneral gathering, and friends brought food and offered their condolences. It seemed that they would never leave, their voices blending into an inaudible sound of platitudes. By early evening, only family members remained sitting on Gramp's big porch, staring at Aunt Cat's favorite chair.

"I can remember that, for most of my life, Catin was like a second mother to me." Ma-ma needed to talk it out. "She was already married when I was born. I was so young when my mother died that Catin stepped in to help take care of me. And I think one reason I married in such a hurry was so that I could leave this depressing house. It changed after Momma passed. Papa never approved of your daddy, but I think he knew I had to leave the house when Momma died. He was old, and I was the last one left." Almost trance-like, Ma-ma continued, "I didn't know what I was doing—I was just doing."

I was speechless. I could see that I had quietly rebelled against marriage all of my life because Ma-ma saw it as a woman's only real option for a successful life. This revelation was powerful and explained so much about my life. I had to wonder if this emotional backdrop to my life had set the stage for my unconscious self-sabotage of my relationships and my selection of men.

The evening was calm and kind, cooler than usual, and comfortable. Ma-ma and I avoided the confusion inside by sitting on the big porch. Ma-ma left me to go to bed. She was in deep grief.

I looked to the sky and whispered, "Aunt Cat, I hope you are not disappointed in me for what I am about to do. I can't wait for your spell. I have to get this monster myself. Peace to your soul, chér. You added so much to our lives." I went inside.

CHAPTER THIRTEEN

The long good-bye ritual was especially painful. I was seeing the family in my rearview mirror as I took a detour en route to Lafayette's airport. I was on a mission. I had made a hasty decision, but it felt like the only good thing to come of this mess with Michael.

I arrived in New Iberia. I had prepared the directions ahead of time to take the rural back roads behind the town. As I stopped and parked the car in front of the old house, I heard the screech of an old screen door as it opened. As people often do in small towns, the woman came out to see who was there.

"Can I help you, ma'am?" she asked, looking down to see inside of the car.

I got out.

"Hi, I am a friend of Michael's. I am in Louisiana for the funeral of my auntie near Franklin."

The woman was about thirty, but she didn't seem youthful. She was like many small-town people who seemed old after age twenty-one.

"I am so sorry for your loss, chér." She had a thick south-Louisiana accent.

"Thank you."

Before I could continue, a child version of Michael ran out of the door and grabbed his mother's legs.

"What a cute little boy," I choked out.

"Oh, thank you, ma'am! He is a handful, yeah." The woman continued, "We wish he could see more of his daddy, but you know, he's a pilot; he stays gone," she said proudly.

"I am so sorry, but I forgot your name. Michael told me and asked me to say hello, but I am sorry, I didn't write it down." I forced a smile.

The woman waved her hands as if to excuse any concern. "No problem. My name is Cheryl Dugas, and my son is Brandon Dugas. You know Michael? Oh my God, that is just wonderful!" She looked down and continued, "Michael and me, we never got married yet, but maybe one day…"

I couldn't bear the woman's shame, so I thought quickly and reached for my wallet.

"Michael asked me to give you this for you and the boy."

I pulled two crisp hundred-dollar bills from my wallet and handed them to Cheryl.

The young woman's eyes were filled with light and tears, and I could tell that the money seemed like a fortune to her.

"Oh, I knew he'd send us something one day. He takes so long to call and to send help, but he says that even though he has a big important job, the pay, it's not so good. Oh, my God, he musta saved up a time for this, yeah. Thank you, Jesus." Cheryl looked to the sky in joy.

The woman grabbed me and hugged me tightly.

"And you come to bring my blessing, even though you are grieving yourself. Thank you, thank you." She continued to hug me.

"Will you be talking to Michael soon?" I began to cover my tracks. Cheryl looked sad.

"Oh, no, not for two weeks or more. He had to fly out of the country, but I'm glad he thought of us before he left, yeah."

"Oh, that's right. He did say he was about to do an international flight," I said.

I suspected Michael must have crafted a lie to coincide with the time of the wedding. The sight of the young woman and the precious boy melted my heart. And I found myself fighting back tears. She was so sweet and innocent. She deserved better. We both did. I sensed a kind and open heart in this woman. She still trusted people.

"I have to get to the airport, but I am so glad I got to meet you. Take care of yourself and that beautiful child."

The woman hugged me again.

"You just don't know how much we needed that money, chér. God bless you for bringing it."

That rotten son of a bitch has someone so vulnerable that she believes all of his bullshit, like he couldn't send money through the mail or a wire.

But then I realized that despite our outward differences in education and economic class, I was not much better than Cheryl. I, too, had fallen for his bullshit. The difference was I had a plan for revenge.

Back in Oakland, I loaded my bags onto the shuttle and was soon in front of my condo building.

I picked a great French cabernet from the wine cabinet, drew a bubbly bath, and allowed myself a long soak. A new thought entered my mind.

After my revenge on Michael is complete, what then? What will I do with my life? Keep singing? What about my practice?

I had routinely listened to many horror stories as a therapist, but no way did that prepare me to experience this kind of tragedy myself. I often encouraged patients to move on, pick up the pieces, and made other trite, by-the-book recommendations. Now I felt guilty and irrelevant. Now, I could truly empathize with my patients and bring more of myself into my practice. Despite this insight, in this moment, I couldn't move on yet.

The next morning presented itself in cruel beauty and insensitive sunshine. I peered through the window wondering how the sky could seem so happy in the company of so much sadness. I thought I saw Corwin and grabbed my phone to call 9-1-1, but the man was too young to be him. I had hoped I was rid of Corwin and could have at least one problem out of my life. Only days from the wedding day, I had an open calendar for the next two weeks, which were supposed to include a festive wedding and a seven-day honeymoon.

I heard the jingle of the key in the door. It was Michael, still believing that his intricately created facade was undisturbed.

"Hey, babe. How are you holding up? I know what Aunt Cat meant to you." Michael almost sounded sincere.

"I'm going to be strong for her memory. By the way, how are your RSVPs for the wedding coming?

"Oh…oh yeah. Fine." Michael stumbled an answer. "Got um…um, but unfortunately with my bad family relations, I don't expect many to come. I'm just happy to be joining your family. It's such a great, close group."

I recognized his attempt to gain sympathy but ignored it.

"You know what? When we come back from the honeymoon, I want to set up a budget for our two-income household," I said.

Michael was obviously caught off guard.

"Absolutely. We have to make sure we save money and watch our spending after this. I have a financial planner who can help us with that."

Yeah, right. He is out of his mind. If he has a planner, why does he need to borrow from me so much, and why didn't I care about that until now?

"Hey, babe. Let's have a really peaceful lunch today. We can invite your friends and their husbands."

Michael's perkiness irritated the shit out of me.

"Well, as much fun as that sounds, I really need to get with Ma-ma these next few days and run through last-minute details. Don't forget we have a rehearsal tomorrow night."

"How could I forget that?" Michael smiled a broad smile. "I am about to have the best catch in the Bay Area as my very own wife."

"I have an idea. In order to make sure the honeymoon is truly special, let's stop sleeping together until after the wedding. You can continue to sleep over at your place, and we can add some sense of tradition to our plans." I was now as good as Michael in faking sincerity.

"I like that idea," he responded.

"It sounds better than waking up together and driving over to the ceremony. I can begin staying at the apartment in San Ramon full-time after the rehearsal tomorrow. I'll move a few more of my things over there. That reminds me, I have to give the apartment manager notice that I'll be moving soon. I hate to break the lease, but no big loss, right?"

"No, it's not, really. But you know, I had another idea. Why don't we keep the apartment and sublease it out to cover the costs? Since it's a furnished apartment, there's no reason to have to move anything. We can just get someone to take it over until the lease is up, and then they can opt to get their own lease," I suggested.

"That's brilliant," Michael said.

His quick agreement led me to believe this somehow worked out for him and his devious plan.

"I can call the manager and take care of it—"

Michael quickly interrupted, "Oh, nooo, your plate is too full now with all the wedding stuff. I'll get that taken care of myself during the week."

Michael left, remembering some papers in San Ramon. I was relieved and prepared to spend the day in my nightgown. I had lied to Michael about needing to meet with Ma-ma, so his leaving worked well. A familiar chill rushed through my head, this time piercing the area between my eyebrows and nearly causing my eyes to tear up. I saw myself with Nikeba, but I don't know where we were.

I shouted to the ceiling, not sure where else to speak to my mystical source. "It almost doesn't matter what you show me now—I'm knee-deep in this mess!"

CHAPTER FOURTEEN

The next morning, I threw on some badly matched running suit pieces and made a mad dash for the tiny chapel I had chosen for the wedding. My mother was already there waiting. She showed no visible signs of her deep grief for Aunt Cat. I realized this wedding was her therapy, and the pride she felt in marrying off her unmarryable daughter made all right in her world.

"About time." She looked frustrated.

"Sorry, I overslept."

"Never mind that. Let's get going with this walk-through before the rehearsal. Now, Sarah, I think we can have the children, the bridesmaids, and you enter from here. The groomsmen and Michael can enter from the front of the chapel." Ma-ma was in her element, blocking out steps and pathways and totally caught up in the theater of the wedding.

I hope my plan for revenge isn't too much for Ma-ma. Maybe the girls are right. I am putting too many others at risk. Maybe I should rethink this whole thing.

I refocused on my mother, who was now walking down the aisle holding imaginary flowers, as if she were the bride.

Jesus. This woman is starting to scare me.

"You're right, Ma; this will work just fine." I agreed to anything, just to end the torture.

I took the rest of the afternoon for some time alone. I walked around Jack London Square, seeing but not seeing, feeling the planks under my feet but not experiencing the wharf. Through my personal fog, I heard my name being called.

"Sarah? Sarah! Over here! Hi there! How have you been?"

I couldn't believe it. It was Lance, Mr. One Night.

"Lance? What a surprise! I've never run into you here before."

"I was in the area and decided to come here to eat and watch the water. Still in the same place and still working at Helmington Hospital. I think about you a lot. You must think I am a terrible coward. I have wanted to talk to you so many times. I would call but lose my nerve and hang up."

I was kind to him. "Lance, I know. My caller ID shows the hospital, and I couldn't imagine anyone but you calling me from there."

"Are you serious? Oh, man. I am so embarrassed. You must think I am an absolute lunatic."

"In my business, there are no absolute lunatics, but I did think it was pretty strange," I chuckled.

"After breaking it off with a voice mail, I was not very proud of myself. I thought the last thing you would ever want was to speak with me. You might find this difficult to believe, but I have trouble with confrontation." Lance held his head down a bit.

I looked at Lance and had no animosity toward him. At this time, I had much more on my plate than a one-nighter who never called back.

"It's OK. I got over it, and I understand. I have confrontation challenges myself."

"But that is what was so bad about it. After that, I had regrets. I dated a few more people and even had an exclusive relationship for a short time, but I never enjoyed their company as much as the night we met. You are so funny and clever and have that unique laugh. I told myself that it was stupid to end it before really getting to know you. I was worried that if we spent more time together, it would be harder to end it and better to just stop it before it started. I just wish I would have waited and given it a bit more time." Lance had deep regret in his voice.

"Well, it is funny how things work out. I met the love of my life, and I'm getting married this weekend. The wedding is this Saturday." I faked happiness.

"Serves me right," Lance responded. "Somehow I knew I was making a mistake but just never worked up the guts to do anything about it. I know staying in touch is out of the question now, but take my number just in case. You may need me for something, and this time, I will be good for it. You deserve a great future. I wish you the best."

I could see that Lance was honestly disappointed.

"I wish you the best, too. Take care of yourself."

I watched Lance walk away. I looked at his card with all of his numbers on it and put it in my jacket pocket. I looked at my watch and realized it was early afternoon, so I was still on a schedule.

I walked inside the condo and could tell Michael had been there because he had a way of moving things. But there was an odd feeling in the place. I walked to the bedroom closet to get a change of clothes for the evening rehearsal and noticed that things were in disarray, as if the place had been ransacked. Drawers had obviously been rifled through because they were open with clothes or items spilling out. The other odd thing I noticed was that all of Michael's things were gone. I looked in his drawers, his closet, and his side of the medicine cabinet. Everything was gone. Even the electric shaver he kept there because he bought another one for the apartment in San Ramon was missing.

I could feel the anger and suspicion boiling in me.

Bastard! He's even going to cheat me out of my revenge!

My heart started racing, and my first thoughts went to my money. I looked for my checkbooks; they were all there. I checked every credit card. They were all untouched. I looked in the place where I kept a thousand dollars in the house as emergency money; it was untouched. I then realized that the jerk had just run out before the wedding. I dialed Michael's cell phone to see what was going on. It had been disconnected. I called his office, and the administrative assistant said he was out for the next two weeks. I was struggling to control the panic in me. I called Nikeba, knowing that with her resources, we could find out what was going on.

"This fucker has disappeared. Gone." I spit the words out through anger.

"What? What do you mean?" Nikeba asked.

"This rotten, fucking, could-be-a-bigamist motherfucker has ditched me before the wedding! All of his shit is gone. All of it."

"Have you checked your money and accounts?"

"Yes. Everything is untouched."

"Let me try to think of what you should do. Give me a minute. This has really caught me off guard."

I could feel the wheels turning in her head.

"His cell phone is disconnected, too! Son of a bitch! This place looks like it was hit by burglars."

"That jerk. Let me talk to Steve. He may have some ideas. I will call Sandy, too."

Nikeba hung up before I could reply.

I went to the living room and plopped down on the sofa. I sat and stared into space. I was not exactly hurting. I was just angry about the lost opportunity to get Michael jailed. I was also confused as to what he was doing. He didn't steal anything. He just up and left in an obvious hurry. I was confused by it all. *What the hell is he up to? I thought his evil plan involved marrying me, but maybe it was to lead up to a wedding and then run? That doesn't make sense.*

The telephone rang. It was Nikeba.

"I have Steve checking out some leads. Sandy and Jean are going to ride out to San Ramon and see if he's at that apartment or if they've moved out of there, too. They will call as soon as they see or hear anything."

"Oh shit. The wedding rehearsal and dinner are tonight! Should I start making calls to cancel?" I couldn't think clearly.

"Oh, damn. Let's see. Ummmm. It's three o'clock. I tell you what. Call your mom and tell her that Michael is running really late and you need to reschedule the wedding rehearsal party from six o'clock to seven thirty tonight. Ask her to make the calls. Tell her that you will be calling all of us."

Nikeba was rushed but planning pretty well.

"OK. I'm calling Ma-ma first." I was a robot.

"Sarah, don't worry. I'm on the way over right now."

"Thanks, Nikeba. I'm scared."

About forty-five minutes later, Nikeba arrived. We hugged.

"No news yet, but what the hell are we drinking while we wait?" Nikeba asked.

"I'm nursing some Jack Daniel's while I sit here."

"Well, nurse, hit me! I'll use this glass." Nikeba grabbed a stray glass that sat on the coffee table.

Time dragged. Nikeba almost dozed off when she noticed it was just past six o'clock.

"Sarah, do you want me to put on some soft music?"

"*No.*"

"TV?"

"*No!*"

The phone finally rang. Nikeba answered. It was Sandy.

"Can you put me on speaker so I can say this once?"

"OK, we're listening."

"Sit down. Get steady. We have horrible, horrible news." Sandy was shaken, and there was fear in her voice.

"*Whaaaat?*" Nikeba and I shouted in impatient unison.

"Well..." Sandy began. "We pulled up to the apartment complex, and there were like four police cars and three fire trucks here, lights going and all. We pretended to be residents and parked the car and walked into the crowd of spectators. We kept asking people what had happened, and then we noticed the door to Michael's apartment was open, a lot of smoke was coming out like there was a big fire, and officers were walking in and out. Two ambulances were also in the parking lot, and I hate to say it..."

"Say what!" I was shouting.

"They're pulling out body bags. Two big ones and one little one." Sandy stopped to sob.

"We don't know yet who's in them; we'll stay out here and find out more. We know it's Michael's place because we had been following him, but I don't think the cops know that yet. Maybe you should turn on the news to see if you get any info. There are a bunch of reporters out here. This is so scary and weird. Let me go to get more information, and I'll call back in about ten minutes. Oh, my God, you guys. This is too much!" Sandy began weeping again and then hung up.

Nikeba and I looked at each other, frozen. I turned on the television.

Some random show was on, but nothing mentioned Michael's family or his apartment complex, and then the program was interrupted. The anchorman's words caused us to sit up.

"Turn it up." Nikeba stood up.

From the TV, we heard: "We will again update you on what appears to be the deaths of an entire family in San Ramon. Details are sketchy, but neighbors say they were tipped off that something was wrong when they heard shots and saw fire. We go now to our reporter on the scene, Leslie Barrett. Leslie, what are the police saying?"

"Well, Dennis, as you can imagine, the people in this upscale community are in shock and wondering what happened to their neighbors. Police are not yet releasing the names of the victims but say it appears to be the badly burned bodies of a woman in her late thirties or early forties and her children. There is the body of a male who appears to have been in his twenties and another child who police guess to be between ten and twelve years old. Police say the father or husband is not at the scene. He has not been seen since the discovery of the bodies, and they have not been able to contact him. While he is not a suspect in the case, they are looking for him as a person of interest. Dennis, that's all we know at this time. We will update you when we learn more. This is Leslie Barrett, KTMA News, live at the Grand Lake Apartments in San Ramon. Back to you."

"Thanks, Leslie, we will check back with you later in the show."

Nikeba and I sat in disbelief.

"Holy shit. Holy shit." Nikeba could only repeat herself; she had no other words.

I started to shake.

"Nikeba. I want to run away."

"Run away?"

"I mean hide."

"Oh shit! You are right. Let's get the hell out of here! As far as I'm concerned, he is a suspect and it won't be long before they release his name and all the details. We don't need to be here or anywhere he could find you."

Nikeba, known for her strength, was shaking, too. We managed to fill two large suitcases with clothes and financial records and headed out the door for the garage and my car.

"Sarah, don't drive your car. We should use mine," Nikeba insisted.

"Oh, yeah, you're right! Let's…let's go." I locked the door, and we used the stairs.

Once in Nikeba's car and down the street, we called Sandy's cell phone. My heart was pounding so loud I could barely hear her update.

Sandy whispered, "Hello?"

"We have left the condo and will find a hotel in case Michael tries to come back. Or is planning to hurt me."

"Good idea. We don't know what the hell is going on here." Sandy whispered to Jean that we were headed to a hiding place.

"We did see a quick news report that police seem to suspect foul play," I shared with Sandy.

"That's the same thing we are hearing out here. They won't give the names, but neighbors of course know whose unit it is. They say he used to beat his wife frequently because they used to hear her screams. They also say the police had come here a few times to break up fights."

Sandy and Jean had listened in on conversations and even managed to ask a few questions of spectators.

"Call us back if you hear more, and be careful, sweetie!" Nikeba yelled into the phone.

"You guys, too," Sandy answered.

"Oh, Lord. Oh, Lord. Oh…" I started to moan as fear took over. I couldn't control my shaking hands or the pounding in my ears. I felt pure panic taking over.

"Look! I love you, but I will slap the living shit out of you today!" Nikeba went off. "We don't have the luxury of a girly panic right now.

Damn it, this is a horrible, horrible thing…but, Sarah, we need to get our asses in a safe place right now. Don't go bats on me right now, girl. Think. Where can we go?" Nikeba had given me a verbal slap, and it worked. "I know. Let's go to San Francisco, a great place to get lost."

"That sounds good, Nikeba, but let's make sure we don't go to any of the places where Michael and I used to go. I think that a hotel would be perfect so I can screen guests and calls. At first, I thought about renting a room, but that's not secure enough." My mind was thinking more clearly.

"True." Nikeba was calming down a bit. "And wherever it is, Sarah, you may have to stay there a few weeks. So, let's go for security."

We drove around the city and settled on the Hammond Hotel on McAllister in the midst of downtown. The area was filled with people and activity.

Nikeba checked in under her name for added protection. We struggled to take the overflowing suitcases to my temporary new home. Once inside the room, we locked and double-checked the locks of the doors.

"Now I better call Steve."

"And I'll call Ma-ma. I'll tell her that Michael's been in an accident, and we have to cancel rehearsal tonight. I'll ask her to make the calls," I said.

I had to convince Ma-ma to just follow my orders. After that, I relived every detail of this grand and now dangerous mess. I felt especially horrible that I had endangered friends and family.

"Well, Steve is calling his friends in law enforcement and giving them information about Michael to help them catch him. Once they have his name, his real name, they can trace his steps by credit cards or practically anything he does. Steve is also going to call Raphael and Jean's husband. He'll get one of them to go to San Ramon to be with Jean and Sandy. He says none of us need to take chances at this point and he isn't that comfortable with us being alone. He will come here after he is finished working with the police."

"Let's keep the news on so we can hear any updates," Nikeba suggested.

We turned on the hotel TV, and it soon became background noise as Nikeba began reminiscing about the tight squeezes we had managed to get into and out of over the years. I knew that she was intentionally recalling every funny story we had lived through to give my emotions a badly needed break.

Nikeba began chuckling.

"Remember that time we tried to get you introduced to that fine fitness trainer?" Nikeba looked up as if that day were playing out in the air. "He was gorgeous!" She reminisced.

"Yes, he was...and remember how we followed him from the gym to his place for three weeks?"

The memory made me laugh.

"And then when we decided to just happen into his favorite deli for lunch..."

"And that beautiful woman showed up to sit with him..."

"...Right before my planned strut to and from the bathroom to get his attention." I got up and mimicked the way I had walked that day.

"Oh, yeah." Nikeba was choking on her laugher.

"You said you'd show him your kick-ass figure, but all you showed him was ass..."

"Yeah, heifer. You could have given me a sign that my dress was stuck in my pantyhose."

Nikeba howled at the memory.

"He looked at you like you were out of your mind. You were doing that *come here* strut, trying to walk sexy with your old tired butt showing, and, of course, you never wear panties, so boyfriend saw it all." Nikeba was nearly screaming with laughter.

"And I had already flirted on the way to the bathroom, so I really thought I had it *going on*." I snorted. "But when I pranced out, a girl was sitting there with him. When you told me the bad news about my soulful strut, it was sooo embarrassing but too funny."

"We left so fast, I think we skipped the check." Nikeba's laugh was winding down.

"Yeah, that ended that crush. I never wanted to see him again in life." My laugh trailed off.

We rejoined our previous silence. We realized that today's event would never become one of those funny stories to look back on. This was dangerous and tragic and more horrible than anything we'd ever known or experienced. This story, should it end safely, would be one to forget. We both fought back tears.

"Thanks so much for staying with me, Nikeba. I have really gotten into a big one this time. I was stubborn and stupid, and now look at us: you're hiding out with me, Jean and Sandy are at a murder scene, and I was engaged to a married maniac who may also be a murderer. They can't write shit this good."

"This one tops them all." Nikeba nodded in agreement.

"Nikeba? Would you mind if I got pissy drunk?"

"Shit, girlfriend, not before me."

Nikeba opened the minibar, and we began our escape.

Nikeba's cell phone rang. It was Steve. She put the phone on speaker so that I could hear.

"Nikki, I have more info for you two." Steve sounded very satisfied.

"I was able to get all of Michael's information to my cop friends, and they got it to the San Ramon PD. Turns out, he tried to buy a plane ticket from the Sacramento airport with his credit card, and that's how they got him. He says they almost had to shoot him to take him in. Let Sarah know he is in custody, but encourage her to stay the night there, just for the sake of peace and to get her bearings. In fact, Nikki, why don't you stay with her; it'll help."

"Thanks, sweetie. Will do. I'll call you later." Nikeba hung up.

I was relieved from the news but still hating myself.

"You can go now, Nikeba. I can stay by myself."

"Oh, no you don't. Whatever I have to do will keep. This is a good sleepover, and you will be paying me back for using my credit card for the room. Let's get back to that minibar and more stories."

"Thanks so much." I wept.

This was one of those times best shared with your best friend in the world, and Nikeba was that friend.

CHAPTER FIFTEEN

Sunlight streamed into the hotel room and found both of us in a deep, alcohol-induced sleep. Neither of us had changed clothes or emptied my suitcases. We were surrounded by minibottles and glasses with melted remnants of creative drinks.

Nikeba and I had let Jean and Sandy know Michael was in custody and that we would stay at the Hammond Hotel for the night. Ma-ma had called my phone at least twenty times during the night, so I was sure that Michael's arrest was now public. And I also had a string of calls from any number of family and friends. Corwin left a creepy message saying he told me Michael would be sorry, and Chico left a message offering to have Michael killed. I erased both equally disturbing messages and ignored the rest. I couldn't even face anyone by phone at this point.

I called Ma-ma and gave her the assignment to let everyone know that I was safe in the city and that Michael was in custody, under suspicion of killing his wife and children.

"Dear God. I never would have thought I'd be explaining that your fiancé is suspected of killing his wife. Jesus, this is just terrible."

"Ma, can you imagine what I feel like? Please let me not talk to anyone today. I need you to make those calls. Please."

"OK, Sarah. I'm glad you are safe. Good-bye."

Steve called to let us know what Michael told the police. He was on speaker on Nikeba's phone.

"He had been questioned all through the night, and it seems like he carefully left out big portions of the story, especially anything to do with you, Sarah. I had given the police the folders of information you guys had gathered on Michael so they knew the whole story and waited for him to tell it all, which he did not. He told them that he went back to the apartment late morning. He was finishing up some work at the office before taking the rest of the week off. He said that he and his wife were preparing for a trip, a second honeymoon, and their oldest son was staying at the house with the younger child."

Nikeba cut in. "No mention of the upcoming wedding?"

"No, Nikeba. Let me finish please, dear. Michael said that when he got to the apartment, it was on fire. The door was open, and everything was charred. He went inside and saw the bodies, burned beyond recognition. The detective tells me that Michael has been crying all night. They believe he is a real sicko but don't want to see him get an insanity defense," Steve finished.

"I think running might ruin his chances at that," Nikeba added.

"Well, did he call the police once he found them?" I asked.

"It seems he did but never said who he was. He said he was afraid. But the police say there is a large chunk of time that Michael cannot account for, and he's not filling in the blanks. But he insists he's innocent," Steve added.

While Steve and Nikeba dissected the legal aspects of Michael's situation, I couldn't help but think of Aunt Cat and how she predicted Michael would meet his deeds—and the way she implied one of her spells may have helped it along.

The news about Michael and his family seemed to be the only story on television, radio, and all area newspaper front pages. My nightmare was now public, as was all of the shame it brought with it.

"You know, I can stay here at the hotel another day; it's no problem." Nikeba made a kind offer, but I could tell she missed her husband.

"No, you have done more than enough for me. I have to face the music, as they say. So you get yourself together and go spend time with your wonderful husband after you take me home, of course."

"OK, OK. Let me shower, and we'll go." Nikeba was half talking, half mumbling, walking toward the shower after opening my suitcase and grabbing a T-shirt and a pair of running pants.

I looked at my friend and felt lucky. We checked out just before noon to avoid additional room charges and left San Francisco en route to Oakland. In the car, the story of Michael and his family was all over the radio. The story was being compared to another domestic tragedy in Northern California in which the husband had a mistress and was the primary suspect in the murder of his pregnant wife.

That shot of reality hit hard.

"Nikeba, I…am the mistress in this case. Shit, I'll have to testify. I'll be smeared all over the news. Oh, fuck! I'm fucked. I can never show my face anywhere again." Pure panic returned.

"Damn, I didn't think about that, but you're right. You probably have phone messages from the police," Nikeba agreed.

"This will ruin me. I'll have no credibility as a therapist after this."

"Try to stay calm. Don't talk to the police without a lawyer. Steve and I will get one for you. Don't answer your phone. Sarah, you have to listen to me about this." Nikeba was firm.

I wasn't listening. I could only hear the pounding in my ears and chest. It had returned. I got out of the car and insisted that I pull the oversized luggage up to my place alone. My voice messages were overloaded. I let the messages play while I tried to make the place feel less violated and more like my home. Nikeba was right. I had a message from the police. I wrote down the detective's number and decided to take a hot shower before returning his call.

"Detective Lang? This is Sarah Doucette Jean-Louis."

"Ms. Jean-Louis, we're gonna need to talk to you sometime today. Where were you?" His voice was harder than his words.

"I was afraid that Michael Rochon would come looking for me, so I took a hotel room in San Francisco after my friends told me that his family had been killed." I tried to be calm but couldn't hide the quiver in my voice.

"Well, we're going to need to know how and why your friends were at that apartment and how all of you knew it was Michael 'Rooshon' before we did." Detective Lang had a warning sound in his voice.

Steve's call to the police had helped them to find Michael but also raised many more questions about how we all knew about Michael.

"I understand. I can be there in about an hour and a half. Is that a convenient time?" I asked.

"Yes, just come to the PD here in San Ramon and ask for me." Lang hung up the phone.

I left Nikeba a voice mail message and left for San Ramon.

The latest newspaper article reported that Michael was scheduled for arraignment that day and preparing to plead not guilty. He also was asking for a court-appointed attorney because he couldn't afford to pay for one.

Not far from the cell that Michael now called home, I was entering the room where I would meet with Detective Lang.

"Coffee?"

"Yes, please, black."

Lang motioned for an officer to get coffee for me.

He closed the door and began rapid-fire questions.

"When did you first meet Michael Rooshon?" The detective seemed to be intentionally mispronouncing the name as he leaned in to me.

I began my long dialogue of an answer, taking the detective from meeting Michael in Louisiana to the engagement. But before I could get to the part about how my friends found out the truth about Michael, there was a knock and the door opened, revealing a stern and ruggedly handsome face.

The attorney stood tall and confident in a deep-navy-blue suit, which was obviously tailored to his buffed physique, a white shirt, and a navy-and-wine-colored power tie. I gasped when I saw him. He was striking.

"I'm going to have to insist that I have time with my client," he broke in curtly. "She shouldn't be here talking to you without representation. I am Manuel Cabrera, retained to represent Dr. Jean-Louis." Manuel handed his card to Lang, who took it and put it on the table without looking at it.

I stared at the attorney, whose sculptured jaw and wavy black hair only added to his Latin charm. His piercing eyes looked at me and through me. The interrogation ended abruptly, and Detective Lang left the room.

"Do not ever, ever talk to the police without an attorney present. This is a murder investigation, a big-assed murder investigation, and you could wind up in prison for saying something the wrong way at the wrong time. All of your words matter now. I am going to work to separate you from that son of a bitch in the minds of the police. And I have to make sure the DA doesn't try to make you out to be an accessory. I don't want to be mean; I just want you to know how serious this is." Manuel's gaze darted into me harshly. His narrowed eyes were filled with anger.

"Serious? How serious this is? It's so serious that I may lose my fucking livelihood and freedom. By the way, I am a family therapist. Let's see how that'll work after this. Serious? I am supposed to be walking down the aisle, but oops, my fiancé is married and, by the way, he may have killed his family! Do you think I have a grasp on how serious this is now? You rude jerk!" I began shouting at this stranger, letting all of my frustrations land on him. And then I did the last thing I wanted to do: I started to cry—not prettily like a girl but a massive snotty slobbering, like a wounded child.

"Hey, hey, I'm sorry." Manuel's eyes softened, and he took out his handkerchief and gave it to me. "I know this is a lot for anyone to handle. I am here to help. I didn't mean to come on so strong. I am going to help you. But you have got to listen and take my direction. That's the only way I can help you."

His voice was filled with concern and comfort. "We'll get that jerk."

I finally felt comfort.

"Let's go to my office. I'll have lunch brought in, and we will officially begin documenting all that has happened."

"OK."

While working my way to 580 and 80 en route to the tollbooth for the Bay Bridge, I began to experience a sense that all of this was happening for a reason. This wasn't a vision, but a sense of knowing something. I couldn't explain it, but I felt sure there was something larger at play. I would suffer for sure, but somehow, it would all work out. This handsome tree of a man made me feel calm and taken care of for the first time in a long time.

CHAPTER SIXTEEN

I stared at the small tray of deli sandwiches. Who could eat? I wasn't sure if I would spend the next years in disgrace or in prison. Or both.

"I'm sorry; I can't eat anything," I apologized.

"I'm not surprised." Manuel kept his protective and comforting tone.

"Maybe as we go over the information, you might get hungry."

"Now, the worst of it is that you and your friends knew Michael was married and you continued to plan a wedding with full knowledge of that. Why didn't you immediately get him out of your life?"

"My answer is not a good answer," I confessed.

"That's OK; just tell me why." Manuel's eyes stared steadily straight into mine without judgment.

"I decided that in order for Michael to be arrested and charged with bigamy, I had to go through with the wedding, and I was going to have police there to arrest him right at the ceremony."

My plan was so lacking in intelligence, I was embarrassed. Before all of this, it seemed to be the perfect, easy revenge. Now, it just sounded stupid and desperate.

Manuel rubbed his eyes in disbelief. He then asked me to start at the beginning again.

I relived the past months, at times bursting into tears. Manuel listened and wrote feverishly. He was recording it all but took notes also. I got to the part about the engagement and the sleuthing by my girlfriends and felt I had to try to make him understand my reasoning.

"I know now that my plan for revenge was not very smart, but I was overwhelmed with pain," I explained.

"Well, I believe we can make a good case for why you are not an accessory. We also can point to Steve's quick action on your behalf by using the information your friends collected to help the police. I have to ask again, where were you on the morning and early afternoon at the time of the murders?"

"I spent the morning at the wedding chapel with my mom preparing for the rehearsal. I left there about one or one thirty and walked around Jack London Square." I was telling the truth, so it flowed easily.

"Did anyone see you at Jack London?" Manuel asked. "Did anyone you know see you?"

I remembered Lance but didn't want to mention him.

"Sarah, I need to corroborate your story of your whereabouts. Think. We need someone, *anyone*, who saw you. I'm not doubting you; it's what we'll need in court."

"Oh, boy. I ran into a guy I used to date. We talked for a while."

"That's great. You are damn lucky to have run into someone. That's just what we needed to prove you were where you say you were at a critical time. Face it. We can assume that the jury will not be predisposed to believe you. They will more than likely believe you are more villain than victim, in cahoots with Michael."

Easy for you to say. I have to humble myself before Lance now. But it beats a prison sentence.

"I'll have to speak with your mother and that friend." Manuel said that once all of our actions had been accounted for and Michael's record of violence considered, things looked pretty good.

"Notice I didn't say easy but *good*. We will need everyone we can think of to testify in the trial. We have to show you as a victim and a good citizen in the community."

"I understand."

By this time, I had faced the fact that I had to humiliate myself to Lance, all friends, and all family. My pride had to be placed on hold until my ass was out of trouble.

The two-hour meeting ended.

"I will be taking statements from your friends, and then all of you will be asked to give your statements again to the police. After that, in about a week, I will meet with the district attorney and emphasize your complete cooperation with the police."

"Any instructions before I leave?"

"Don't talk to the police about the case unless I am there with you." Manuel smiled.

My God, he is gorgeous! What kind of sick am I? This is not the time to acknowledge an attraction.

"Sarah, I'll call you with updates on the situation as I get them. And don't worry. I'm here for you."

I couldn't even remember driving home but fortunately made it there. Shortly after I kicked off my shoes, the phone rang. It was Ma-ma, of course.

"Sarah, why don't you come to my place for a few days?"

"No, Ma, I'm fine. I do have to tell you, I just met with my lawyer and you will be called upon to testify in Michael's trial."

"*Jesus*, Sarah, I thought this thing would be over. None of us had anything to do with this. If I were to have anyone killed, it would be that Michael, but no one in our family would hurt children, not even with spells, *fi pitan*." Ma-ma cursed in French when she was extremely upset.

"Ma, your part is mostly to help clear me. Your testimony will prove that I wasn't anywhere near Michael's apartment but with you that morning. I have another friend who saw me at Jack London right after that," I explained.

Ma-ma reluctantly accepted the realities of a murder trial. She knew that I was in too deep for her to protest. And while I was on a roll, I called Sandy and Jean with the same bad news of their need to meet with my attorney. Steve and Nikeba already knew, so I didn't bother to call them.

I poured myself some juice, plain juice with no alcohol, and went to sit and take in all that had changed in my world. Something kept telling me it would all be fine. I found that hard to believe but couldn't shake that feeling. Maybe it came from a deep place within where hope originated. Hope was all I had to hold on to as the next few weeks would unfold, so I embraced it hard.

I stared at the two-week-old manicure on my fingers and tried to buy time. But the truth was, I had to make the call. I wondered if there were other words for ultimate humiliation, when you'd made a complete ass of yourself at the same time someone was making a complete ass of you. I needed that word. I needed to figure it out before I called the man who slept with me once, dumped me, and apologized while I gloated about getting married to a murderous would-be bigamist. I needed a big word for that. My head spun with the dizziness of one of my visions. The brief, colorful sensation was me smiling. I was walking in a beautiful garden. It was almost cartoonish with bright colors, flowers, and sun. It was very childlike. I was childlike and happy. I was so very happy. Again, my vision was more filled out than before and, more important, I could feel my emotions in the vision. I understood now why Aunt Cat, like Carl Jung, felt feelings were more important than facts. Feelings could reveal what words could not.

The rings seemed endless.

"Hello?" a pleasant and unsuspecting voice answered.

"Lance, this is Sarah. I hope all is well with you…Lance, something very serious has come about, and I have to speak with you as soon as possible."

There was a brief silence.

"Sarah, I heard about it on the news, and I am so, so sorry that you are at the center of this horrific case. I wanted to call but did not know if you would want to talk to anyone right now."

"Yeah, I guess the only ones who haven't heard of this case by now are indigenous peoples in rain forests, right? Huh…" I faked a fake laugh.

"Sure, if they do not have cable." Lance was funny. It was a comfortable geek-like joke for Lance. He could easily relate.

"Lance, my attorney needs to establish where I was at the time of the murders. It seems that I was talking to you at Jack London Square at that time. I'll understand if you want to stay away from me and all of this. I just—"

Lance stopped me as I tried to continue through audible tears.

"I will testify. I will help you. You do not deserve this; no one deserves this. Every time I read something about the case in the paper and see you and your friends' names mentioned, I cringe. This must be a nightmare. I will help. Just tell me how and when."

My heart opened. This peculiar nerdy man, after all was said and done, wanted to help me. I gave him Manuel's phone number.

"You can call him at your convenience, and he'll tell you what he needs from there. Lance, thank you so much. I...I...can't thank you enough." I sobbed rhythmically.

"Don't worry, Sarah. We will all help you. We will."

I snorted a good-bye, and Lance hung up.

CHAPTER SEVENTEEN

The Contra Costa County courtroom was buzzing with reporters, curious onlookers, and Michael's and my family and friends. It had been several weeks since Michael's indictment for the killings of his family. I noticed a group of unfamiliar faces, and it didn't take me long to realize the group included Michael's parents and siblings.

After all witnesses had been sworn in, the bailiff led them out so they could wait to be called upon to testify. Michael's court-appointed defense attorney, Chris Jansen, spoke with a passion that came from his voice, not his face. He gave Michael's version of the story and chose to paint him as a disturbed man whose destiny had never been in his own hands. He explained that he was trapped in a loveless marriage and had succumbed to its pressures. He accounted for Michael's whereabouts and actions that Tuesday and framed the entire story with Michael's sad attempt at a second honeymoon with the woman he felt doomed to share the rest of his life with. The jury seemed faceless to me as they listened, showing no reaction.

Deidre Herman, the prosecutor, stood and faced the jurors. She was a forty-something white female taking the lead on this high-profile case. Deidre Herman was a gifted speaker and an even better attorney. She was venomous in her description of Michael as a man who lied to women as a matter of habit and abused them once he had gained their confidence. The jurors bristled at the photographs of the crime scene and the bodies of Denise and the children, lifeless and burned beyond recognition.

"This man would have you believe he was a victim." She pointed to Michael. "But was he a victim when he proposed to a woman while married to another? And let's not forget the child he fathered while married to Denise. Trapped? Is the defense trying to imply that his feeling trapped was justification for his actions? We say no. Emphatically no. Fortunately, we don't live in a society in which a man can put away a woman when she is no longer deemed useful or she prevents him from having a new life. We live in a society in which bad marriages can end in divorce but do not have to end in murder. And when we begin to fathom the evil that would lead this man to kill his wife, we are further disgusted by his attack on his very own children. Not only do we believe that Michael Rochon is guilty of a murder that he tried to cover up by setting fire to the scene of the crime; we also believe he is a danger to society, especially to the women who would be or could be future targets." Deidre then took her seat.

Manuel was sitting directly behind Deidre. He had done all he could to help prepare my friends and family for this day. He felt hopeful but was prepared should any of us need his services as a result of this trial.

Ma-ma was called first from our group. The prosecution used her testimony to set the stage of my relationship, engagement, and wedding plans as a way to tell their story of Michael's preparation to get rid of his family and begin a new life. Ma-ma was very controlled. This was one time I was glad that my mother was not a very emotional person. I knew that she would be precise and not break, even under cross-examination by the defense.

"Didn't anyone in your family ever ask about Michael's family?" Michael's lawyer worked to establish the fact that no one in my camp knew much about Michael but failed to try to find out more.

"We often asked about his family," Ma-ma replied. "My daughter passed his excuses along to us. We never accepted those excuses and felt we should meet his relatives before the wedding, but we respected Sarah's wishes and let her handle it. We never would have imagined he was much worse than a con man." Ma-ma was firm.

She shot the last sentence out before she could be stopped by an objection from Michael's lawyer.

"Objection, Your Honor, the witness has no proof that Mr. Rochon is a con man or anything else." Jansen was quick to his feet.

A few snickers could be heard from courtroom observers.

"Objection sustained," came from the judge. "And we will have order in this courtroom. There is nothing in this case to laugh about." The judge spoke to the filled room.

"Move to strike that last remark, Your Honor." Chris Jansen was doing his job as Michael's counsel.

"Granted. Ladies and gentlemen of the jury, you will disregard the term *con man* in the last testimony."

Jansen soon realized he was no match for Ma-ma. She was an older woman who looked soft but talked tough, and he could tell the jury loved her immediately. During the next few days, Deidre's next witnesses were people from Michael's office, former employers, apartment managers, and police officers who had been to his home on domestic violence calls. Nikeba took the stand and in thirty minutes of testimony gave jurors all of the drama, suspicion, and sadness my friends had experienced. She shared the contents of her folder on Michael, facts they pulled together, and the method they had used to gather them.

"What about the day of the murders?" Deidre asked slowly, giving Nikeba a great amount of range with which to answer questions.

"When Sarah called in a panic saying that Michael had removed all of his things from her place, we, her close friends and employee, decided to try and find out what was going on. We were not sure what he was capable of doing and wanted to find out where he was so Sarah would not be further victimized."

Nikeba's training as an attorney was evident.

Deidre then asked, "And did you ever find Mr. Rochon?"

"No, Sandy and Jean went to his apartment complex while I stayed with Sarah. The two called us immediately after arriving at the crime scene. At that point, Sarah's safety was our first concern. While they stayed at the scene, I helped Sarah pack a bag so she could find a place to hide from Michael." Nikeba placed added emphasis on "from Michael" so it would not be assumed I was running from the law.

Jansen's attempt to show that Nikeba could not account for her actions before going to Sarah's condo failed miserably.

Sandy and Jean gave similar testimony. And Chris was just as unsuccessful in implicating them in the murders. The jurors seemed unresponsive. They wore blank, emotionless poker faces.

On the fifth day of the trial, I entered the courtroom with my new-found and undesired celebrity. Stillness came over the room when I walked in. I was surprised at how kind the jurors seemed as I spoke.

Deidre was skillful at getting the basic, factual questions out of the way before asking her killer question.

"You are a brilliant woman, a family therapist, and affluent. How could you plan a wedding and know so little about this man?"

I took a deep breath and shared my truth.

"I believed I had found love at first sight. I believed that I had to get married. Not because of a pregnancy or anything like that, but I believed that somehow with all of my success I was still a failure because I had never been married or had a child." My testimony brought it all back.

"I had a quiet desperation and didn't try to find out why Michael had so many secrets. I guess I assumed that if he did have secrets, they would be relatively harmless, like bad credit or a history of being a player. Once I learned the truth, I stupidly thought I could have him arrested at the wedding. My reasoning was that he would not officially become a bigamist until after the wedding. I wanted him stopped and thought an arrest and subsequent jail time would do that. I realize now that this was a flawed decision, but I had no idea any of this would happen. I feel so sorry for everyone involved. And I do now realize how deeply disturbed this man is."

Jansen shot up from his seat. "Objection, Your Honor, Dr. Jean-Louis is not here to testify as an expert; she is only here to explain her role in this."

The judge instructed me not to attempt to give a psychological analysis of Michael as part of my testimony because I had not evaluated him in that way and could not serve as an expert witness.

I nodded.

"I had no desire to see anyone harmed or killed; I just wanted Michael to go to jail and be stopped in his predatory ways." I made myself clear.

Judge Vinton Hanover was an elderly, been-around-the-block judge. He had served on the bench for twenty-five years and was extremely short of patience and tough on defense attorneys. Judge Hanover let me finish my statement and then called for a short recess for lunch.

I chose to spend the lunch hour continuing to clean out my office. Jean told me she believed the practice would pick up again, but I had already lost nearly all of my patients because of the news stories about Michael's murder trial and my status as the mistress in the case. The first clients I lost were those awarded by the civil courts. I gave Jean six months' salary and decided to close the office, at least until the end of the trial. All my office attracted at this point was random reporters. After lunch, it was time to return to the courthouse and the witness stand. But to my surprise, I was only asked to give ten more minutes of testimony. While on the witness stand, I noticed a woman whose dark glasses, hat, and attempt to cover her face made her stand out. And, of course, Mr. Corwin was in the audience each day. He looked as eerie as Michael, with wild, uncommitted eyes and misplaced smiles.

Jansen's cross-examination was very brief. The last prosecution witness from my group of friends was Dr. Lance Gaston. His calm testimony gave an accounting of my whereabouts at the exact time of the murders. Deidre then focused the subsequent days of the trial on the police and medical examiners' testimony and tied a neat package around Michael as the killer of his own family.

The trial seemed to move along at a pace of its own, fast and deliberate. Soon, it was time for closing arguments. Deidre gave a chilling account of the murders, asking jurors to imagine the bravery of a twenty-one-year-old young man with his whole life ahead of him deciding he would shield his younger brother from his parent. She then asked jurors to imagine Denise's face as the only man she ever loved was getting rid of them all permanently. All of the years of abuse could not have prepared her for the brutality of this. Denise's family members, Michael's parents, and many members of the jury wiped tears as

137

Deidre concluded her dramatic closing argument, inventing the final hours of the family in great detail.

"All the while, the defendant was anticipating his new life. He would start fresh with a wealthy, successful woman. He would begin his life anew. He would erase his bothersome wife and burdensome children and begin a privileged life with Dr. Jean-Louis. She was the perfect partner for his escape. All he had to do was gain his freedom. And, ladies and gentlemen, that's what he did with the oldest line in the book, 'an intruder killed my family.' How stupid does he think we are? He killed his wife first and then shot his children and set the apartment on fire. You heard the testimony of our experts. He needs to be stopped for good. I ask you to punish this heartless and cruel man. He should not be allowed to hurt again, to kill again. Stop Michael Rochon. Thank you."

The defense counsel seemed defeated before he began.

"Ladies and gentlemen, this is one of the worst tragedies our community has ever known. It is not often that an entire family is slaughtered. But we cannot let our pain cloud the facts. The fact remains that my client was at his office on that fateful day and did not return home until after the crime was committed.

"The fact remains that while my client was a master of deception, he has never had the capacity for murder. And he would never, ever take the lives of his own family. Remember, he had plane tickets for a second honeymoon. Why would he have made plans for that trip with his wife if he were planning a murder? Let's not create another tragedy by convicting an innocent man of something he did not do. He has not been a model husband or father, but he is not a killer. Allow this man to get the help he needs, because that need is now deepened by his grief at losing all of his family. Ladies and gentlemen, don't make the mistake of blaming him because the system failed to find the real killer."

Jansen was attempting to appeal to reason, and jurors seemed to be caught in emotion. Once they were read the charge by Judge Hanover, the jurors left to deliberate.

With the trial ended, my condo became the gathering place. The atmosphere was a thick blend of tension and relief.

"I sure as hell hope you have learned something from this," Ma-ma started with a tone of harsh judgment. "This is just horrible, and I can't believe it has smeared our family name all over the media."

I was in shock. A dark feeling that combined sadness and outrage swirled deep within my stomach. The anger that came with it traveled up my spine and came out of my mouth.

"I don't believe this. This is inarguably the worst...worst time of my entire life! And you don't think of me...you think of all of you! You know what? This is not the time to blame me. Maybe it's the lifetime of blame and shame that I seem to have caused you that led me to so desperately try to get a husband. Why am I never good enough? Everybody in this room has your approval but me. My perfect, orderly brother and his perfect life escape judgment and receive constant praise."

Lyle flinched a bit upon hearing his name.

"My difficult but tolerated sister who managed to nab a caretaker in the form of a husband is applauded for that pile of dysfunction." I pointed to Lizette.

Lizette opened her mouth to voice an objection, but her husband, Tom, shook his head and silently formed the word *no.*

"And let's not forget those not present but accounted for because they did what was expected of them and married and had children on schedule. Well, dammit, I'm not taking all of the responsibility in this. I am not the villain! I am the victim, and forgive me, Ma-ma; I am fucking tired of bearing the burden of my unfortunate circumstances. I appreciate the public support, but I resent, absolutely *resent*, the private scorn. I don't deserve it, and I will no longer accept it. This party is over! Please, all of you...just leave!" I had crossed a line of something but couldn't stop myself.

Ma-ma gathered her purse and her dignity. Her jaw was tight with anger, and she refused to speak. It was the classic Ma-ma shutdown. She left with Lyle, Lizette, and their families.

Once empty, my place seemed to hold me and bring the comfort that none of them could. I had no idea what would be next in my life, but I knew it damn sure would not include tolerance for unfair judgments, not even from Ma-ma. We call it breakdown before breakthrough, and it was my year to hit all of the biggies. I had the classic paradigm shift and would no longer accept family, men, or friends disrespecting my boundaries. There was no turning back for me. I would no longer be the one others put down in order to feel better. I knew that powerful, successful women could make family and friends uncomfortable and insecure. They often react to that by honing in on flaws and perceived weaknesses. It was their way to find that hole in the armor. That shit was over. I would turn the spotlight right back on them and force them to face their insecurities. From then on, the therapist would push the freakin' buttons! And I'd do it with skill.

The jury deliberated for two days, and all were called to return to the courtroom to hear their verdict. By this time, I was still not communicating with family and friends. I sat in the back of the courtroom, next to the covered-up lady in the big hat and sunshades, in order to leave quickly. The press had enough bad pictures of me.

"All rise, the Honorable Judge Vinton Hanover presiding," the bailiff opened up.

Judge Hanover turned to the jury forewoman, a stately woman with a handsome face and salt-and-pepper hair.

"In the case of the *People versus Michael Rochon*, have you arrived at a verdict?" The judge's words took little effort.

The woman stood and answered, "Yes, we have, Your Honor."

She handed the verdict to the bailiff, who handed it to the judge.

"Will the defendant please rise?" The judge silently read the verdict and then spoke to the forewoman. "What say you?" Judge Hanover asked.

All I could hear was "…find the defendant, Michael Rochon, guilty on three counts of murder in the first degree."

Michael's mother wailed. Denise's parents sobbed. Michael bent over and moaned. He was removed from the courtroom after the judge told him when he would be sentenced. I left the courtroom quickly. I felt vindicated and a sense of relief I had never known and I hoped I would never experience again. I was exhausted. Spent.

CHAPTER EIGHTEEN

Back at home, I began serving a self-imposed life sentence. I closed myself off from everyone.

The next few days were a series of sunrises and sunsets that I hardly noticed. This was unusual for me because I was ordinarily fascinated by the sun, the clouds, and the sky and opened my heart to their greeting every morning. A few days after Michael's sentencing, I read the words in disbelief. Michael was sentenced to death. The newspaper story gave the sentencing, the verdict, and a full accounting of the crime with several mentions and photos of me.

"Cheers," I raised my glass. "Couldn't happen to a better man. Now you can hurt like the rest of us; in fact, before they kill you, you can suffer like the rest of us while you wait."

I looked over the wedding invitations, the wedding gown, and my ring. I cried so hard I thought my head would burst. A strong vision began to reveal itself in my mind's eye. This one came in without the sharp pain and nausea. I could see a crazed woman shooting children. I saw another woman's body and a fire being started. She went through great pains to set fire to the woman's body first.

"Oh, my God! Michael didn't do it." I was talking aloud to myself.

I closed my eyes to hold on to the vision and the moment of revelation. I could hear Aunt Cat's voice, not orally but in the spirit sense, like a sensation. Usually, the sensations of my meditations gave me the essence of words but not a recognizable voice. I seemed to be entering new spiritual territory with the voice of Aunt Cat.

"No, chér. He didn't do it. But know this, he was planning to kill you and stay with that woman. You were in danger, chér. You will learn more about that danger."

In the past, Aunt Cat had told me that she often heard spirits and angels in sensations that formed words. I knew now that I was taking my rightful place as owner of the truly developed gift of visions.

My spirit was renewed by this new level of experience. I called everyone I could think of to apologize for my anger and bitterness. I started with Ma-ma. She was stoic in her acceptance of my apology.

"Ma-ma, I'm sorry."

She was quiet.

"Ma-ma. You can't understand what life is like for me. I'm blessed, but I am as challenged as I am blessed. This situation took everything out of me. It will take a while for me to fully recover. I couldn't take criticism. I just couldn't."

"Maybe I understand more than you'll ever know, Sarah. But a mother forgives."

"Merci, Ma-ma."

She hung up.

I realized that Ma-ma had done all she could do. I didn't push because forcing her to accept some of the responsibility of my choices would have been unfair and impossible for her to do. It wasn't in her makeup to accept blame. *A daughter forgives, too.*

I told Nikeba some of my vision.

"Nikeba, this is urgent. Can you meet for lunch?" I was determined to act on this insight.

Nikeba agreed. I dressed and went down to my garage. I could tell someone was there but couldn't see the person. I rushed in and locked my car doors. There was a piece of paper on my windshield. It read, "You should have died, too, bitch." I grabbed it with a scarf of mine that was on the passenger seat. Thanks to movies, I was cognizant of fingerprints. I decided to give it to Nikeba for Steve to have investigated with his contacts. My hands shook with fear. My stomach was upset with terror. *Will my life ever settle down?* Other than Corwin or some other nut motivated by my media coverage, I had no idea who this could be. *Will I ever sleep another night?*

"I still say that Corwin freak is upset that you closed the office for a few months. I was never comfortable with him," Nikeba said.

"Maybe so, but it's creeping me out. Anyway, I know you don't respect my visions much, but I need for you to listen to this. Here's what came to me yesterday."

I told Nikeba the entire scenario of a woman committing the crime and that it was revealed to me that Michael was planning to kill me and stay with Denise.

"Sarah." Nikeba stared at me wide-eyed.

"What?"

"There is no way for you to know this, but I know that after the trial, Michael told police that he was planning to kill you, take any and all of your money he could get, and then go on a second honeymoon for an alibi. I guess that was his way to clear his conscience before facing his maker. My God, you really do get this stuff! You really get messages. How? How in the hell does this happen? There was absolutely no way for you to know that. You haven't let any of us near you. And the last thing I wanted to do was call and tell you this because you had been through enough already. Oh, my God. You really have this gift thing! How exactly does it work?" Nikeba was shocked.

"Well, it's not an exact science, and the visions don't come in as precise as I would like. Sometimes I get a sensation. Sometimes I hear words—not through my ears but from within. I can't explain it." I tried to articulate the feeling of it all with Nikeba.

Nikeba didn't even blink while I explained to her the entire history of my visions and how they had evolved.

"Sometimes these brief scenarios appear in my head. That's when I get those flashes. Sometimes they come with colors, and sometimes they just hurt a little. Once the flash passes, I see a scenario briefly."

"Wow! This is amazing."

"Nikeba...You will think I'm crazy."

"Honey, that train left the station long ago."

"Seriously, there is something I have to do. I have to prove Michael's innocence."

"Oh, puh-lease. He may not have committed this crime, but he can't be called innocent. Plus, Sarah, he is still a dangerous man," Nikeba reminded me.

"But my gift requires me to work for revealing truth. Even if it doesn't get him off, so be it. I have to try to reveal truth," I insisted. "I have time on my hands. The only patient who would even consider coming to my office is—"

"Let me guess, freaked-out hat man. The stalker."

"Yes. He says he will wait for my office to reopen, if it takes forever now that Michael is being punished. He left that message last week."

"Be careful about that nut. And I'll see if we can tie him to this note from your car."

"Oh, I'm more paranoid now than I've ever been. But because I have this, uh-hummm, free time, I thought I could at least try to get the real story out."

"Well, I have no idea how you can do that without being locked up your damn self."

"Truthfully, I have no idea either."

A few days later, the idea that came to me for clearing Michael began with Manuel.

I sat in the lobby of his office, and as I reached for a magazine, I saw him appear out of the corner of my eye. He was just as tall and electric as he was the first time I met him. Manuel took my hand and placed his other hand on top of mine.

"It is good to see you, Sarah. You look great."

"Thank you and thanks so much for making time for me. I know how busy you are. We don't have to go out to lunch—"

"No we don't. Lunch is being brought in to us. Sushi OK?"

"Sushi. My favorite. That's great," I answered.

Manuel led me to the conference room, and we sat across from each other at one end of the long marble table. I wasn't sure how to begin, so I just dove in.

"Manuel, I have…I know…well, you see, it's about Michael. I…let me start from the beginning…"

The verbal dive was bumpy. I decided to explain my gift of visions from childhood up through my most obvious examples of spiritual intervention. "The visions began as just brief scenarios. They also were preceded by physical symptoms like nausea and violent ten-second headaches. As I became older and more spiritual, I noticed that the visions expanded. This year, emotional interpretations were also revealed. I can now interpret them better than ever in my life. They carry prophecy and spiritual messages to help me navigate my life. My aunt was a master with this gift. I don't have her ability yet."

By the time I brought Manuel into current revelations, I insisted that we get Steve on the phone to verify Michael's intention to kill me. We put him on speaker.

"It's true, Manuel. Sarah's gift is uncanny. There was no way for her to have known that Michael was planning to kill her. I can't reveal how I know this. I have a source that will remain confidential."

"Thanks, man. Appreciate it."

"OK. Talk soon."

Steve hung up.

Manuel was calm. The concept of visions didn't seem to be totally foreign to him.

"Sarah, how much control do you have over this gift?"

"Well, not much, but it is evolving and strengthening."

"I'm not sure you can help Michael, but rather than taint your gift on him, you might be able to help in other cases."

"What do you mean?"

"I mean, you are a trained therapist with an extrasensory gift. You could be even better than a police psychic."

"But I'm not psychic; I am an intuitive. I channel spiritual voices and insight. I have visions of what has been or will be, sometimes in code and not always as obvious as a video. You think I could solve crimes?" I was curious.

"Well, maybe not solve them, but certainly add insight on the really difficult cases. Sarah, in my culture, there is a lot of candle-lighting, so this is not so far of a reach for me. But when a good Jewish boy like Steve believes, I'm ready to get on board. This gift can help so many people." Manuel was serious.

I was both surprised and relieved that my gift was being accepted as a legitimate tool rather than just Louisiana hocus-pocus.

"I will set up a confidential meeting with a friend at the Oakland Police Department. That would be a great start. Sarah, this could be great. As for Michael, sorry, I won't be part of anything for him. I just can't."

We finished lunch with a lighter conversation, and Manuel walked me to the elevator.

Once in my condo, I went for the window to close the curtains and caught a glimpse of someone in a heavy gray overcoat with a knit cap and a scarf nearly covering the face. The figure stared at my window and didn't run away as Mr. Corwin would do when discovered. This person was bold, and I had a sense of hatred and evil coming from him or her. I kept staring also in order to seem brave, but inside, I was terrified. I called Nikeba so that Steve could have an officer come over to check it out. I sat for a meditation and asked for answers while I nervously waited for the police.

If I had to make sense of my year of turmoil, I would say it was necessary to grow me emotionally and spiritually. This was the year to fine-tune my gift of visions and to increase my emotional maturity for my future relationship with a man. I'd grown leaps and with much pain. The vision was a strong one. I saw Denise place another woman's body in the apartment, set the fire, and run away. Somehow I knew the shadowy figure appearing lately was Denise. I never truly thought it was Mr. Corwin. I called Nikeba and Steve to share this. I needed their clout with the police. I needed the dental records or some DNA proof that the woman in the fire was not Denise.

"Sarah, Steve said the best they can do is try to prove that the person stalking you is Denise, rather than to prove the corpse is not."

"OK. How in the hell do I do that?"

"We have an idea, but it's a bit scary."

"And what is it?"

"You become the bait to out Denise."

"What?"

"Sarah, if she's after you, you are already the bait. And lately, she's becoming bolder."

They set up a meeting with a female detective at the police department. I sat with my elbows on the table listening.

"The next time you see her, yell out that you want to talk. Once you make the arrangements, we will have you wired with these, and the police will be nearby your meeting place."

My dignified composure was broken. "Oh, hell no! I'm a decoy? Hell…nooooo."

"Sarah. It's the best way to make this truly bizarre case. We'll be all over the place." The detective was working me.

What next this year? Locusts?

She talked me off the metaphorical ledge and managed to get me to agree to set a trap for Denise. Something within me wanted to solve this case. I was terrified, but I was the only one who could do it. I had to stop overanalyzing it, or I would refuse. I wore the wire every day. I jogged around the lake, walked to stores, and generally made myself available to a woman who could possibly be a murderer and seemingly wanted to add me to her list of victims. The police were always in plain view, but that didn't make me any less nervous. *Talk about your pushed times.* Only Nikeba and Steve knew this was happening. I kept to myself for the next few weeks, refusing lunch dates from Lance and invitations to go out for drinks from Sandy and Jean. I even turned down brunch invitations from Ma-ma twice. I couldn't risk their safety in all of this. I found myself on a mission with a new passion for revealing the truth. Not surprisingly, our manipulation paid off one Sunday afternoon. I was walking around Lake Merritt, wired for sound. I felt

149

someone mimicking my steps. My walking pace remained while my heart raced. I didn't turn around.

"Sarah, you disgusting, man-stealing slut. Don't turn around."

There were about ten or fifteen people out around the lake, but I felt alone.

"Who is this?"

"None of your business who this is. Have you gotten my notes?"

"Yes, uh, Denise, I got them."

"Who told you it was me?"

"I just had a feeling. Do you want to talk?"

"Yeah, I do want to talk. I have some unfinished business with you, and if you don't come, I know where your mother and all your friends live. I've been following you for a long, long time, Sarah."

"When do you want to meet and where?"

"I'll put a note on your car. Just keep walking. I'll be in touch."

It was as if I had held my breath the whole time. I exhaled and ran home.

"Well, she doesn't have a tap on your phone. Since we do, we would have picked it up. Just let us know when you get the note, and remember, we will be with you, Ms. Jean-Louis," the police officer assured me.

I had never been this afraid. I double-checked all of my locks before going to bed. And even with my deep fear, I wanted to get it over with and have Denise as locked up as Michael.

Denise made good on her word. My note for a meeting was placed on my windshield the next morning. It said, "Bring your ass to the white house at Tenth and University in Berkeley tomorrow. It's right on the corner. Get there at ten in the morning. I'm waiting for you." I told the police, Nikeba, and Steve. I said a long prayer and moved into action. Our meeting was for the following morning.

Why did I let this crazy bitch talk me into meeting her? Not to mention that female detective with the sun-worn face.

But I knew she had threatened to hurt Ma-ma, and after she killed her own kids, all bets were off with Denise. I slowed down but knew that I couldn't turn around. I had committed. I had been wired by the police in my most private of places and hoped that the sweat wouldn't embarrass me later—if I had a later. I was meeting a demented woman. Despite my profession, I had never faced this much danger. I was much too proud to let my life flash before my eyes, so I chose instead to think about Aunt Cat, the warmth of her apron, and the great smells that came from her kitchen. I imagined her watching over me and saying, "Don't let dat sorry bitch scare you, chér. We got something ready for her up here, yeah." I immediately felt stronger with an inexplicable sense of calm.

The condemned-looking, crumbling two-story, wood-frame house and its concrete steps would stay in my mind for the rest of my life, however long that would be. My hesitant steps were outpaced by a nervous mind racing to make sense of a woman who rationalized killing her children and likely had me next on her list. I'd never had a patient with this level of criminal insanity. I had arrived at the meeting place. I walked up the concrete steps to the front door and pushed it open with my left foot, leaving my right foot ready to stomp her ass. But no confrontation met me at the door. In fact, I looked to the left and saw only a badly stained wood floor that had the memory of wax in spots. I looked to the right and smelled only dust and mold. I leaned inside a bit more and looked deeper to my right and almost behind the door I saw an old blanket shaking. Denise was leaning against the wall, her feet on the floor and her knees bent. She was crying, shaking, and holding on to the old musty blanket that covered her knees.

"You took too long. I was tired of waiting for you!" Her voice was hoarse and shaky and reminded me of the drug addicts I had worked with over the years.

"Denise, I came as fast as I could—"

"Don't. Interrupt. Me. I am so tired. I am so tired of all you perfect women. You look good; you talk good. You got your education and loose morals and take any man you want to take!"

"Denise. No one took Michael from you. Michael strayed. Let's remember what has really happened. Let's—"

"Don't give me that therapist shit. Let's kiss my ass! My life was fine until all you man-hungry whores started cropping up around me and my family."

Denise trailed off into another place when she heard herself say the word *family*. She whimpered like an ailing puppy, and for a few seconds, I felt sorry for her. I wanted to help her, but when I was about to reach toward her, the shine and reflection of something caught my eye. It was like a small mirror, but no such luck. Denise pulled a large chef's knife out from under the blanket. She looked at it and smiled at her reflection in it. She slid her fingers up and down the smooth wooden handle, following the flow of every curve.

"This is my favorite way." She coughed and tried to clear a raspy throat.

"Way to what, Denise?" I struggled to make my voice louder than the pounding in my heart. I tried to keep my eyes on her every motion. No surprises please.

"Stop saying my name. I'm not one of those stupid people who pay you to listen and do nothing! Stop saying my name."

"OK. Well, let me just help you with this situation. We don't have to be angry at each other. We both were victims in this." My training was the only thing helping me to get through this. I was about to pee my pants.

"Oh, yeah, cuz we're all in this together. You fucking fool. Don't you understand? I am in charge of this, *all* of this. I decided to get pregnant on that worthless fuck. Then, when he couldn't keep it in his pants, I decided to take care of the ones he kept around too long. Do you know that he used to call me all of the names of those women while he fucked me? He would name the whole list and name a different name with each stroke. Then he'd call me a washed-up, used woman who couldn't get another man if I begged him."

Denise seemed to be in another place, almost talking to someone else. Her face, hands, and head were animated with big gestures. I kept my eyes on her hands and that knife.

"He would do awful things to me. So I fixed him and all of his bitches. That dumb one in Louisiana was easy. I told her that I was

152

Michael's sister. She was really ignorant. She opened the door to a total stranger." Denise shook her head and finger as if to Cheryl.

"You should never open your door to strangers, you stupid little country girl. I told her that I wanted to surprise Michael and bring her to California for a party for him. I told her to let that little bastard stay with her family while she came to a great big surprise party in California. Idiot. We got off the plane and laughed and talked. She told me all about Michael and how busy he has been, so he couldn't see them but once a year. We got out of the car and went into the apartment. She put her suitcase down and said, 'Is the party today?' That's the last thing she said. I got her right in the back. And I turned it."

Denise turned and pushed the knife into the air, reliving the moment. "I only had to keep her hidden a day or so, and then I used her body in the fire. Everybody assumed she was me. I had to put my children down. We had to move on to a different life without Michael…"

Denise trailed off again as if in a daze, and then she gained a rapid focus on me.

My sense was to remain quiet and let her talk. But she stopped.

"Your turn!" She lunged at me with the strength of a man. I held her forearm and even dug red lines into it with my nails, but she never even flinched. She was within inches of my stomach. *Where in the hell are the damn cops?* I was able to turn Denise's arm over her head and around her back. The knife was now facing me, but she wasn't. She kicked my shin, and the pain sent a sharp wave through my entire leg, forcing me to let go of her arm. We faced each other in a strange kind of standoff, and Denise started brandishing the knife in all directions. She yelled, "Yes, yes!" with each lunge. The tip of it caught my forearm, and blood poured down my shirt and onto the floor. I looked at the blood and felt the rush of a feeling I had never known—a perverse, overwhelming joy at the danger. I felt a deadly calm, a certainty that this woman who had cut me, scarred me, deserved to die.

I tackled Denise around the waist and knocked her down. I grabbed for her arm while she stubbornly held on to the knife. But I used my own body, on top of her, to overpower her and wrenched the knife

153

away to point it at her neck. I would like to believe I was stronger, but something told me she gave up and I aided her suicide. I felt a lessening of her resistance and almost her guiding my hand to push the knife deep into her neck. The blood flowed freely and was everywhere. Like ineffective clockwork, the police stormed in, guns drawn. They were listening to everything and still managed to storm in late.

"Do you guys ever make it on time?" I asked. Then I fainted.

Epilogue

Ma-ma and I walked to our first-class seats and settled quickly. For all of the months of bad press, I was now a hero in the Bay Area. Denise was dead, but it was proved she was a serial killer going after women in Michael's life. The murder charges against Michael were dropped, but he faced charges of conspiracy to commit murder, among others. He confessed and pleaded guilty.

"Sarah, I am so proud of you. I could never have done what you have done or what you are doing. You are a great woman," Ma-ma smiled.

She was rarely emotional, but she wiped a small tear from her eyes with her old-school, lace handkerchief. This was evidently a break-through year for Ma-ma also. She actually praised me for me, not in relationship to a man. The ordeal had an impact on Ma-ma and her belief systems.

"Well, I learned from the best that sometimes in this life, there are pushed times and we are sometimes called upon to do things we ordinarily would not. This is the time for me." Ma-ma nodded in agreement and sipped her coffee, while I raised my champagne glass for a toast. Our first stop in Louisiana would be to begin setting up support and education funds for little Brandon, Michael's son. And we would take him to play with the dozens of children at our Godforsaken reunion.

"Besides, chér, this will be the best date I've ever had at one of these horrible, burdensome family reunions." I winked at Ma-ma, and we both laughed.

My cell phone rang just before we were asked to turn them off.

"Hello?...Oh, Manuel...Yes. Absolutely. I'll be returning in about a week, and I would still love to hear all about it...Sure, I'd love to meet over dinner...OK. See you when I get back."

"That's that good-looking lawyer?" Ma-ma asked.

"Oh, Ma-ma, listen to you. Yeah, he has a case that I might want to help out with when we get back." I had a brief flash of a vision. My left hand sparkled with a clean and clear engagement ring. Interesting...

Ma-ma's voice broke through the vision. "Catin would be so proud of the way you are using your gifts and bringing dignity to spirit gifts. But what are you going to do with two men. It's kinda whorish—"

"All right, Ma-ma, remember, I'm from a different time. I am in no hurry to make up my mind. I could do a lot worse than a doctor and a lawyer. Laissez les bon temps rouler, chér!"

"Oh, Sarah. You are so much like your father." And, in a rare and unbelievable moment, Ma-ma and I agreed!

Pushed Times, Lache pas la Patate
(Hang in There)

When I was two, I ate a cigarette and then threw it up. I had raided the ashtrays after a party my parents hosted. My adult life played out that same way—want, acquire, then purge. I was a strange kid who would go on to live a scary-book life. C'est le vie.

Prologue

The staleness in the room made the air feel like wet newspaper. It smelled of death with a Jack Daniel's chaser. I wasn't sure why the room was familiar to me; I couldn't remember visiting it. The walls were dingy gray and sea-foam green. There were thinly blanketed cots against the walls. My inner eyes scanned the place. Another vision elbowed its way into my mind's eye: a man's hand opening a medicine chest. Although I couldn't see his face, I was terrified.

Woooh!

Chest heaving, I jumped up from the dream-based vision with a head full of dull pain. I looked around my bedroom for signs of moved furniture or an intruder, but there was only the faint stream of streetlight angling between my planter's shades, which created a pointed dart on the wood floor. The rest of the room was dark with the eerie peace of my spirit life. *Mo pa konmprann.*

I could almost hear my late aunt Cat's voice saying, "Just hold tight, cher. Da gift will always lead you to what you need to know. You will understand, cher. You will komprann."

I hope you're right, Auntie. I need to know a lot.

By this time, I had accepted the fact that my gift of visions was not to be ignored. The visions presented themselves as new chapters, opening the path to another life journey. I just hoped this time, I could avoid the threat of death.

Chapter One

I liked the theme song of the Wicked Witch of the West from *The Wizard of Oz.* I used it as my cell phone ring tone. It broke into my meditative Sunday morning at home in Oakland's Lake Merritt area. I had filled my condo with the sweet smell of lavender candles and incense, Gregorian chants and the repeating sound of water in my fountain. Those days, I had a lot of time to meditate. My family therapy practice had cratered under the afterglow of my scandalous personal life, and I wasn't sure what I really wanted to do.

I answered the phone and hid my irritation. "Hello?"

"Sarah? It's Manuel."

Manuel was the only thing I was sure that at some point, I wanted to do. His voice caused the backs of my knees to tingle. Although no longer attorney and client, we had kept our chemistry to harmless flirting.

"Hi, Manuel."

"How was the reunion in Louisiana?" he asked.

"Pretty good." I realized I was stuck in nervous, two-word answers.

"Sarah, like I told you before you left for Louisiana, I want you to work some cases for me. Little did I know I'd have one helluva case by the time you got back. Are you game or are you planning to reopen your family therapy practice?" Manuel asked.

"Hah. What practice? I'm still the psychic freak whose patients left when she was outed as the mistress at the center of a murder. Remember?" I giggled.

"Oh, good. You're available," Manuel joked.

"Still sensitive, I see."

Manuel's humor was sarcastic and delicious. But his voice quickly turned serious. I could tell that this case was personal. "I need to meet with you to give you more details about this one. But here's the gist; my partner's son is being framed for a murder I am sure he didn't commit. Sarah, I gotta help this kid. He has a history of drugs, but he has been clean for a year. This situation is so fucked up, I'm not sure where to start. I have great respect for your ability to see beyond the facts. I need that and all of your skills to help my investigator. There's a complexity to this case that I don't think he'll get."

There was true sadness in Manuel's voice.

"Manuel. I am not sure how or if I can help, but you know I'll try," I said.

"Can you meet me for dinner? I want to fill you in," he asked.

"Of course."

"Meet me at Tony's Beach restaurant tonight in the city. I'll have a quiet table at seven. And, Sarah, thank you. This kid is worth it, and I do believe you can make the difference for him."

"Sure. See you at seven." I hung up.

I released my legs from lotus position, and as I stood up, my head swirled. Colors flashed between my temples, and nausea pierced the back of my tongue. It was one of my now infamous visions. I watched images in black and white stream through my mind. Evil, soulless eyes seemed to stare straight into mine. They disappeared. I refused to let the chill climbing up my back disrupt my glass of wine and quality time in my closet. My custom closet was the envy of all friends and haters. My clothes collection was the source that nurtured my tattered ego. I wanted Manuel to remember I had a body riding under my intuitive, five-dimensional mind, so I went for clingy with taste and quickly laid out a dress, shoes, and jewelry.

Sunday afternoons were reserved for my girls. These martini-laced lunches were my therapy.

"I told Steve that I want a real vacation this year. None of this Napa shit, I want an airplane involved. We work, work, and cheat ourselves when it's time to play." Nikeba was firm but not angry. She and her husband seemed to enjoy fake, not bitter, anger. I had never witnessed harsh words between them in more than twenty years.

The subject of time off came up as Sandy spread out family photos of blue sky, a flawless beach, and laughter in her images from Cabo taken during their family vacation.

My mind drifted while I looked at the pictures. My engagement party and dreams of a family life were less than a year ago. My fake fiancé, Michael, was now serving time for attempted murder and big-amy, for living continuously with me while married and with intent to commit fraud. I had come so close to living my dream only to land back in the seat of the fifth wheel.

"Sarah? Sarah!" Nikeba raised her voice. The diners of Sea-son's Restaurant in Jack London Square glared at her.

My attention rejoined the table.

"Oh. What?" I asked.

"Steve's prison contacts say that Michael's been asking about you."

"Really? Why?"

"Hell if I know. I told Steve you didn't care." A vodka-rinsed Nikeba shook her head yes but meant no.

"I wonder what he wants?" Sandy leaned into the table and whispered, as if anyone knew or cared that we were the stars of last year's local scandal.

The patio seats at Sea-son's were perfect for staring into the water of the Oakland/Alameda estuary to San Francisco Bay. Nikeba and Sandy's debate of whether I should visit Michael at the prison moved into a distant background. I wasn't sure if I was inspired by the Kettle One and Castelvetrano olives or nursing a mild depression, but I stared backward to the time of buying my wedding gown and invitations. I smiled remembering Ma-ma and me giggling like children at the cake tasting. And I felt the knife-sharp pain of learning Michael was married and his family had been murdered. I squeezed one year into a few seconds, and my heart sank into the memories.

"You know?" Sandy asked.

I had no idea what she was talking about, but I answered anyway. "Oh yeah. You're right," I mouthed. "Hey, guys. I didn't get to tell you I have dinner with Manuel tonight so I need to leave early."

"Oohhhhhh, ahhhhhh, Manuel," Sandy sang.

"Silly. It's business," I said with a smile.

"Business? What kind of business?" Nikeba asked.

"He thinks I can help with some cases." I reluctantly shared.

Nikeba was a hard-core attorney herself, and she and Steve had known Manuel for years when they recommended he represent me last year. I didn't want to hear her warnings. But she surprised me.

"Good idea, Sarah. I think you need something to dig into," she said.

"I really do. I've been bored. I've been spending a lot more time with Ma-ma, so you know it's time for me to have something else to do." I laughed.

"Whew. You definitely need a project." Nikeba whistled.

"He is gorgeous, too!" Sandy's comment was a bit too loud and a little random.

We laughed.

"Yeah. He is fine. But he's a player. That's all I'll say." Nikeba held back uncharacteristically. She was also tipsy. "Can we get three coffees?" She motioned to the waiter.

He nodded.

"Who said we wanted coffees?" Sandy playfully argued.

"Drink coffee, you lightweight. I don't want Steve to have to get both of us out of jail today."

"Well, I need to go and sober up at home. I think this case is a killer—no pun—and I want to be straight. Sandy, take my coffee. Gotta go. Love you guys!" I gave the royal wave and left.

"See ya!" my girls yelled in disjointed unison.

The valet pulled my shiny black Mercedes up. I tipped him and drove up Broadway toward home.

As I approached my garage, out from a bush jumps crazy-assed Mr. Corwin, shouting, "You can't leave me! You can't leave *me*!"

Mr. Corwin was my former stalking, deviant patient who refused to accept the fact that my practice was now closed.

I rolled down the window and shouted back, "I will call the police on your crazy ass if you come near my home again. Get the hell away from here!"

"You are a professional; you're not supposed to call me crazy!" Corwin shouted while running away.

As I drove under the iron gate into my underground parking lot, I had to laugh out loud. That lunatic was actually right; as his former therapist, it was inappropriate for me to call him crazy—to his face.

Jesus. Corwin today, Manuel, tonight. The forecast for the coming year seemed to be mysterious, murderous, with a touch of crazy. Damn...

Made in the USA
San Bernardino, CA
21 August 2019